DEADLY
Entanglements

DEADLY
Entanglements

MICHELE LEE

Archway Publishing books may be ordered through booksellers or by contacting:

Archway Publishing
1663 Liberty Drive
Bloomington, IN 47403
www.archwaypublishing.com
844-669-3957

Because of the dynamic nature of the Internet, any web addresses or
links contained in this book may have changed since publication and
may no longer be valid. The views expressed in this work are solely those
of the author and do not necessarily reflect the views of the publisher,
and the publisher hereby disclaims any responsibility for them.

Any people depicted in stock imagery provided by Getty Images are
models, and such images are being used for illustrative purposes only.
Certain stock imagery © Getty Images.

ISBN: 978-1-6657-1360-3 (sc)
ISBN: 978-1-6657-1358-0 (hc)
ISBN: 978-1-6657-1359-7 (e)

Library of Congress Control Number: 2021920517

Print information available on the last page.

Archway Publishing rev. date: 11/16/2021

◇ Deadly Entanglements

I HAVE A PERFECT LIFE! WELL, ALMOST PERFECT, I MEAN nothing is perfect, but my life is pretty damn close! I have everything a woman could ask for in life. I'm forty and fabulous! I have a successful law firm, an adoring husband of fifteen years and four beautiful children! My husband Keenan is a well-respected and widely sought-after architect with a very lucrative company expanding from our hometown, the great city of Chicago to the eastern seaboard. His headquarters is in Minneapolis, Minnesota, our newly adopted home state. We have identical twin sons, Keenan Jr. and Keevan 12, and daughters, Kendra 8 and Kyela 6.

If life wasn't busy enough, we extended our family lives to include two English Cocker Spaniels, Bonnie & Clyde! We have a beautiful 6,800-square foot, 3-story brick home on approximately ten acres in the affluent suburb of Minnetonka. We added a three-season enclosed patio facing the pool for those long winter months as it doesn't get as much use as the indoor patio. We are in Minnesota after all!

We are black, successful and damn proud of it! Even more than that, we know who we are, where we came from, haven't forgotten it though I have to remind my husband of this, often as of late. Being a successful black couple doesn't mean you have to give up your blackness!

Its 5AM and the weather is still cool this time of year. No surprise in late April, we're still wearing winter gear! Today is definitely one of those days I would love to stay in bed and cuddle.

"Keenan, honey it's time to get up!" For the life of me, I will never understand why I must wake this man up to get him going and have been for the past twenty-one years! Yes, twenty-one! We moved in together our freshmen year of college, and it's been this way since. You would think he has an auto alarm would be in his head by now! Maybe he just likes my voice better than the sound of beeps. "MyeZelle, I told you last night I took the day off. I gotta meet with Brad Shapiro from Shapiro Architects out of Memphis. The further south I can get, I can eventually start branching out west. Justin is handling everything today. He's in town and if things go the way I plan, he'll be inviting me to join him on some projects in the mid-south."

I'm already out of bed and walking across the room into the master bath before he finishes his long, winded explanation. Of course, he didn't tell me he was taking the day off last night and if he did, hell I don't remember. I work ten-hour days, deal with four kids (five including him) and two dogs. I have come to rely heavily on my House Manager, Rosie to handle the day-to-day operations more recently. Honestly, I have enough bullshit to deal with on a day-to-day basis without being Kee's personal wakeup call!

I absolutely love my primary bath. It's my favorite room in the house. It has a spa like setting that oozes calmness and serenity. Its job is to get me going with good vibes or everyone in the house will feel my wrath until we part for the day. If you can't tell already, I can be a real bitch when things don't go as planned. Hence, the successful lawyer that I am! If I don't argue with you until you're out of breath and completely exhausted, I will ignore your ass until you decide to agree with me! Either way, I win. And in my profession, it's all about winning!

I love the feeling of a hot steamy shower after a restless, sexless night. The shower is Italian marble on three walls with dual rain shower heads and head to toe massage sprayers. Where the fourth wall should be is all glass and overlooks our garden and pool area. A large bay window completes the look. It's my calm before the storm and chaos of courtrooms and undisciplined clients.

I'm not sure what's going on with my husband, but whatever it is, he needs to work it out! I'm tired of excuse after excuse as to why he's not blowing my back out on a consistent basis as of late! You would think I've gained a hundred pounds over the years but that's not the case at all! I'm 5'8", thick in the hips with a nice plump ass. I have a pretty, round face, green eyes, nice full lips and long hair. My breasts are 38-C and yes, they could be firmer and slightly bigger if you ask me but if you're a naturally beautiful woman with a fat ass, men trip over their feet for you! Keenan hasn't received that memo, I'm guessing. My husband just doesn't seem to be that into me anymore so I'm all but certain there's a size 3 white trash whore somewhere on his agenda. I don't bother to ask him why we aren't as intimate in the bedroom anymore, though I'm always trying to spice things up. Now, I just get myself off in the shower or bath. Sometimes it's better that way, at least I know I'm guaranteed an orgasm!

I gave our landscaping crew quite the show last summer though I didn't realize until it was over! I'd had another restless, sexless night and couldn't wait for morning to come. At the crack of dawn, I eased out of bed and rushed to the primary bath because I knew I was about to release a lot of pinned up tension! I was so anxious to fuck myself; I never bothered to look out over the garden, and it was just as well. I reached for Mandigo in a side drawer, propped myself in the bay window and let Mandingo go to work! By the time I climaxed, and opened my eyes, realizing how obscenely loud I had become. I looked out over the garden and noticed the landscapers staring up at me with their mouths wide open! For a split second, I wasn't sure of what to do! I was completely embarrassed and ashamed of myself, but only briefly. Then I thought about it. If Keenan would make love to me on a regular, I wouldn't have given Juarez Landscaping a show that morning! Once I'd gotten over my initial embarrassment, I did exactly what any desperate and horny wife would have done, I gave their ass an encore! I placed my wet ass back unto the plush cushions that sat on the bay window, pressed my back to the wall and spread my legs without ever looking back at the audience below. I pulled Mandingo back out, stuck it in my mouth like it was a lollipop, in and out, in and out, slowly licking the tip, running my tongue from the shaft to the head, used my fingers to play with my pussy like a tongue until I couldn't take it anymore! Finally, I placed Mandingo inside, turning the vibrating motion on full blast until I damn near fell out of the window from gyrating so much! Needless to say, the landscaping to our home became the envy of our small neighborhood and we suddenly became VIP customers with loyalty discounts! It was a win-win for everyone involved, especially me! I didn't realize how turned on I could become from someone watching me pleasure myself into a heavenly bliss!

Today was another one of those days! But I was too pissed off to get off! I could have slept another hour if Keenan really would have told me he was taking the day off from the office to meet with some asshole from Memphis or wherever the fuck he's from. Whatever his problem is, he needs to fix it! I don't have the energy for this shit this week! I have too much going on at work to dwell on Keenan. Our anniversary and my birthday are coming faster than I have time to plan! They're both a few weeks away, and planning for me is everything so yeah, I'm definitely in bitch mode this time of year and lack of intimacy is only elevating that mood!

"Well, since your schedule isn't that busy today, do you think you can make it down the hall to get the kids up and ready for school?" My tone has quickly put Keenan on defense. "Yeah, MyeZelle! Damn, anything else?" Since the asshole asked, "yes, can you also make sure they have breakfast, a hot one and get them off to school? I have to be at the courthouse early and that would help me out a great deal." I can tell by the look on his face he wanted to be out the door as soon as I left. Too fucking bad! I'm taking my time getting ready this morning! "Yeah baby, I can do all that for you," he smirked. I would have kissed him to start something if I thought he was truly sincere but, I knew he wasn't so fuck him!

I obsess with organization in everything I do; an organized MyeZelle usually makes for a happy and pleasant MyeZelle, in most cases. My closet is arranged by designer, wardrobe style and color, same with the wall of boots, pumps, sandals, and handbags. Its 49 degrees and I didn't get any extra warmth last night or this morning to take the chill off! It's a J Crew day for sure, something warm! Think I will go with the deep navy cashmere blouse and pinstriped boy blazer and pants, leather Christian Louboutin boots and a simple Berkin bag.

I'm in the middle of oiling my body down when Keenan walks in rushing me, "I thought you had to be in court early?" Excuse me, I thought, I can't get any attention from you physically or otherwise and you have the damn nerve to raise your voice to rush me out of our house?! "I will be early, earlier than I am any other day and what the hell is up your ass this morning," I snap back! He looks at me as if I'm the devil, makes a quick u-turn out of the bedroom and back down the hall to the sounds of Bonnie and Clyde barking and jumping around. I can't put my finger on it, but something is up with my husband, and I don't like it one bit!

I speed my pace up, get dressed and out of the bedroom rushing downstairs to the kitchen with a sense of urgency. Keenan has already dropped the troops off and pulling into the garage as I finish my coffee and kiss Bonnie and Clyde goodbye for the day. "Baby you were gonna leave before I got back and got some sugar?" He has to be kidding me, right?! If looks could kill, my husband would be lifeless on our garage floor right now, "I got your kiss right here Suga," tapping my ass while walking away! I don't look back to see his stunned face. I jump into my dirty gold BMW X2 and hit reverse before he can plead his case for me to stop. Good thing he hadn't closed the garage as I never looked back before hitting the gas!

The drive to the courthouse in downtown Minneapolis is smooth sailing. I can drive the speed limit out of mostly "White-Man's Land" Minnetonka and into the parking garage of the Hennepin County Courthouse in under thirty minutes with traffic! Minneapolis is a very diverse city in many ways, but in professional circles, our skin tone is in the very low minority! Luckily for me, I'm a damn good criminal defense attorney with the ability to attract rich and wealthy clients of all races, ethnicities and backgrounds. I only take cases of clients who can handle my fees without asking Mommy and Daddy for loans. My clients include professional athletes from all sports: football, basketball, baseball and yes, even hockey!

I don't discriminate so long as they're money is green and long! I also work with Fortune 500 companies and several entrepreneurs who've taken their skills of "hustling in the hood" to wall street and other legal ventures. Most of the stuffy assholes who work downtown require my legal services when their "Becky" has either cheated, spent too much money and gotten their ass beat for it. Lately, I've had a lot of "Karens", these entitled white bitches who think they're above reproach even while being recorded and shared on social media for millions to view! They're often captured berating a person of color demanding to know why they are in a certain place or calling the police because they "fear for their lives". They're mostly "MAGA" supporters who feel is their duty to put blacks and other minorities in our place. Their hotshot husbands then seek my help to, "make the situation go away". Do I defend their lily-white asses, yes, do I tax that ass severely, hell yes! I also get the occasional exec whose used his expense account to provide for his "sugar baby" and gotten caught! It's a very interesting career, never boring! You get the latest and greatest gossip of the upper echelon of Minneapolis and the affluent suburbs while getting paid. Its fucking awesome, I can't lie!

Whenever I'm stressed, I take the longest route in. Driving in morning traffic can trigger road rage in some motorists but not this Queen! I play my favorite artist and allow my mind to shut everything out and groove to the soulful, bluesy voice of the one and only "Mr. Johnnie Taylor".

Unfortunately, I spent too much time getting dressed and under my husband's skin this morning to take the scenic route, but I still have "Johnnie" for a short while. Its 494 North to 394 East now, oh well! It never fails, I run into one or two motorists who have no business driving a toy car, let alone driving on an expressway! I never understand why a person living in one of the snowiest cities in America can't drive in a light drizzle. We live in Minnesota! God forbid, we were still in winter right now! If you can't drive, dammit call Lyft or Uber, or work from home!

"Good morning Mrs. Washington." "Good morning Carla, how are you?" Carla is the sweetest deputy in the Hennepin Municipal Court building considering the bullshit she must go through each morning searching folks and making sure they aren't trying to blow our asses up Monday through Friday. I look forward to her each day I enter the "Nuthouse" with that sweet smile on her face. But don't let the smile fool you, she's not a pushover and handles the assholes swiftly and accordingly when they are out of order! I know I always feel a little better once I see her smile. Hell, if she can still smile, I have absolutely no excuse! I was fourth in line to be searched last week when a blonde "Karen" pranced her ass up to Carla. "Good morning Ma'am", can I have you place your purse, coat, keys and any other metal objects into the bin and step through for me", Carla asked politely. This broad is outraged at the thought of placing her faux mink; knock-off Louis bag in a bin someone else's belongings were in previously. "I can't believe you people want me to put my belongings in this filthy box!" "Ma'am, if it was up to me, you could walk right through," Carla chuckles and smiles as lily "Karen" walks through huffing and puffing. I'm in deep thought about how I could never work a position like this without being behind the same bars I try to keep my clients out of. What a bitch! I hadn't noticed I was no longer waiting in line and Carla was patiently waiting on me to snap out of the zone I was in. We exchange our usual pleasantries, and I'm on my way to see my client, Mr. Ronald Henderson aka "Murder 1".

Ronald is an entrepreneur. He's a legitimate businessman for the most part, at least the only part I need to know as his lawyer. The part of his past he chose to share with me is both interesting and heartbreaking. He started hustling at age thirteen after his parents were tortured and shot to death in a home invasion on the north side of Minneapolis. Ron escaped out the back with his seven year old sister and three year old brother while the intruders were busy torturing his Mom and Dad. He got into trouble a few times while he struggled to take care of his younger siblings. They stayed with a crackhead aunt for about six years. It was all good for Ronald to hustle so long as Auntie Crackhead could get high off Ron's supply. Though I don't totally agree with his methods of survival, I damn sure understand the brother's struggle! By the time he was twenty-three, Ron had gotten a cover job as a bouncer, and was able to move him and his siblings into a modern four bedroom bi-level home in Robbinsdale, Minnesota, and purchase a new Cadillac SUV all in cash! A couple years later, Ron purchased a sprawling ranch home in St. Louis Park he allowed his aunt to stay in once she completed a year long stint in rehab. Shortly after, Ron allowed his younger siblings to settle back in with his Aunt so he could focus on his many businesses. Ron kept the Robbinsdale home for himself as it's a short distance from his businesses downtown though he's rarely there.

After bouncing for several clubs and strip joints, he obtained a nightclub of his own and shortly after acquired a strip club as well. The man is a 24/7 hustler, and I don't knock him. After everything he's seen and gone through, he's definitely a great success story! By the time he turned thirty, he was a multimillionaire.

I notice Ron down the hall, near the courtroom doors once I exit the elevator. As I approach him, that beautiful smile he has makes me melt just a bit on the inside. "How are you Mr. Henderson, how are you holding up," I ask with a nervous smile. He's thirty-five now but a very mature thirty-five, very cool and collected and his swag radar is off the charts. I don't think I've seen him out of a two thousand dollar suit but on the rare occasion my girlfriends and I pop up at one of his clubs. What I can't figure out, why isn't this guy already married or at the very least has a steady girlfriend. "I'm good MyeZelle and I've asked you to call me Ron, if that's too hard, call me Ronald but I prefer Ron." I'm a consummate professional and I never have an issue explaining to a client as to why I don't want to be on a first name basis but he seems to get a little more comfortable with every meeting which makes me a little more uncomfortable. "Mr. Henderson," I can't get my nerves together, maybe too much coffee, "MyeZelle, please call me Ron, its only one syllable," he chuckles.

I escort Ron into a small conference room to go over his case. We both sit and as I'm discussing the prosecutor's case against him, this young man is glaring, almost salivating like I'm a piece of Sweet Potato Pie! This is exactly why I stopped meeting Mr. Henderson at my office, there is no expectation of privacy in a conference room at the courthouse! The past few weeks, I've been contemplating my law partner and best friend taking over Ronald's case. The more time I spend with this man, the more I become enamored by him. I know he wants me, and he knows that I know! What's worse, he thinks he knows that I want him just as much and he's somehow convinced himself that he can have me. It's as if I have a sign on my forehead, "I need a good fuck Ronald"!

Mr. Henderson listens as I explain his case which is flimsy at best and the options to put this behind him. Ron starts to speak and as I try to concentrate on everything he's saying, I find myself daydreaming about what it would feel like to "go there" with him!

"Fuck me Ron, take me on top of this conference table right now! Open my blouse, rip it off! Unfasten my bra and let it drop as you suckle my hard nipples. Rub your hands over the front of my pants, unzip them and pull them to my ankles. Lift me onto the table and lay me out like dinner! Spread my legs like an eagle's wings and dive in head-first. Stick your tongue deep inside my pussy and taste my juices, pull it in and out teasing me. Lick all around my outer pussy lips as I play with my breasts as I moan in ecstasy and beg for you to insert your huge dick inside me!"

"MyeZelle, are you okay, you look like you're in another world?" Hell yeah, my partner can have Mr. Henderson, I can't be in the same room with this man, even if we are in a damn courthouse, it's a wrap! I've worked with Ron for a couple years now and with no love from my husband, his mere presence over the past few weeks has me feeling and thinking thoughts a wife should never think about another man. "Um no, yeah I mean, I'm fine. This case against you really has no merit. Today, I will ask the judge to set a trial date. Should the prosecutor ask for another delay, I will implore the judge to dismiss the case with prejudice. Should it not go in our favor, I think Victoria, my partner should handle your case going forward. I have a trial coming up that will require my total attention and time, so I need to focus on that case as it's far more serious than what is required to have your case resolved. That being said, your case likely should be over today, are you ready Mr. Henderson," I ask nervously. Ron now has the face of a man who's been told it's over by his girlfriend! "Look MyeZelle, I don't want Victoria or anyone else working my case but you. Are you afraid of me or something? I won't bite you, unless you want me to," he ended with a sly smile. I danced around the last comment with blah blah bullshit until it was time to go into court and try to get his case thrown out. Once the Judge gave the prosecuting attorney a stern warning but another continuance, I reiterated to Mr. Henderson I would get Victoria up to speed on his case and hightailed it out of the courthouse as if it was on fire! Now I just have to figure out how to get Victoria on board with this change and keep her nosy ass in the dark about why I'm making this spur of the moment decision, though I'm almost certain she already knows!

Attempting to get Ron out of my head, I give my husband a call to try and "make nice". "Hey babe, what are you doing," attempting to put on my sweetest, sexiest voice. "Nothing, what it do?" I cringe whenever my husband tries to get in gangsta mode. "Keenan, I apologize for this morning, I had a lot on my mind dealing with a case, so I just wanted to say I'm sorry." I'm waiting and waiting on a response. "Oh, yeah baby, it's all good!" I still can't figure out why each time I try to have a decent conversation or offer a sincere apology to Keenan, he totally dismisses me! "Kee, I need to make a quick run by the office, and I will be home by 3, 4 at the latest." He doesn't bother to say, "hey I forgive you", just "a'ight, see you when you get here!" That's it, that's the response I got! He's such a fucking asshole!

My office is on some next level type shit! I renovated it from a dusty artist's loft into a serene, spa type setting with a jungle theme. I installed several tinted skylights in the client waiting area. It has fourteen hundred square feet of open space. The wood detail is impeccable, natural wood beams on the eighteen feet ceilings makes the open concept appear larger.

We brought in live palm trees from Miami and added 3-D epoxy flooring showcasing beautiful beaches and plants the world over. Victoria and I hired a designer who completed the office of our dreams with the purchase of a couple large plush sofas and massage chairs. Adding five feet, electric Hacienda candle stands with soft vanilla and lavender scents makes the office feel more like a healing center. You would never guess it was a law office walking through the glass doors. It's a total Zen atmosphere!

Our thinking has always been, clients coming through those doors are obviously stressed so having them in a calm state would better serve both the clients as well as Victoria and myself.

"Victoria, meet me in my office, we need to talk." My partner knows that look all too well. "Here we go, what is MyeZelle's ass up to this morning," Victoria mumbled. "Sit down, I need to talk to you about one of our clients, well one of my clients." I have a feeling she already knows where this conversation is going. "MyeZelle, which client are we speaking of exactly?" After I danced around the true reason I couldn't or wouldn't be Mr. Henderson's lawyer anymore, Victoria finally agreed. Thank God that's over! Now all I have to do is get this man out of my head and convince him that Victoria is just as vicious dealing with prosecutors and getting clients off as I am!

Victoria and I are practically twins, completing each other's sentences and knowing exactly what the other is thinking. Though she didn't pepper me with questions, undoubtedly, she's thinking there's much more to the story that I'm willing to divulge currently. Either way, she's on board with handling Mr. Henderson going forward and once I convince Ron it's for the best, I can stop daydreaming about this man!

After returning some clients' calls, responding to emails and relaxing on the fire red king sofa in my office to settle my nerves, it was time to blow this popsicle stand. I need to get home to my troops and hubby. I will give Ron, "Mr. Henderson" a call in a bit to give him the news.

Feeling that I'd gotten a load of bricks off my shoulders, I decide to stop by my favorite lingerie shop to pick up a little something for my honey. I'm hoping this will put him in the mood, it damn sure better! I love coming into Laced-Up Boutique to view the latest and greatest THOT gear for an evening in.

The ladies know me by name and always have a nice, chilled glass of bubbly waiting as I always phone first. Hell, when you drop stacks each visit, one should expect nothing less! "Hey Jackie, what do you have in here to blow my husband's mind tonight?" With my birthday and anniversary coming up in a few weeks I will also need intimate wear for those very special occasions. "MyeZelle" Jackie exclaimed, "here's your Sangria my lady. How many prosecutors cried going against you today," she jokes. I smile in return and we both burst into laughter. "I have ten sets picked out for you in all your favorite colors, hills and or boots to match." After a couple glasses, fourteen outfit changes, I settled on the ten Jackie originally picked, the hills, boots, a couple came with whips and other gadgets and trinkets to get Keenan back in the mood! I think Jackie is more in-tune with my freak level than my husband!

By the time I pull into the garage, I'm feeling really, really good! "I'm home everyone!" My girls always greet me first. "Hi Mommy," beams Kendra and my baby, Kenya is right behind her, "hey Mommy, I love you!" "I love you girls too, are you both working on your homework?" I notice Rosie"s busy preparing dinner as we enter the kitchen. "Where are the boys," I ask my daughters. "They're in the game room with Daddy, Mommy," they say in unison. "Girls get your homework completed and Dad and I will check it after dinner." "Yes ma'am," they say, again in unison! I think they have practiced this since they were little because the twins almost always speak in unison or complete each other's sentences. I find it adorable! I kiss my princesses, give them a tap on their bottoms and head downstairs to the game room.

"Hey honey," greeting Keenan in a low sultry voice! "What's up boo, missed you," he responds. Wow, what a change in tone from earlier I think to myself but I'm definitely here for it! I can smell cognac on his breath so he's feeling something! "Hey Mom," the twins yell while playing Fortnite, not bothering to look up. "Hey boys," as I walk over to get my kisses. "How was your guys' day at school, where is your homework and is it finished?" Keenan answers before the boys have a chance, "yeah baby, I checked their homework, and they are good. I just let them get a game in before dinner." If so, why aren't the girls' homework completed and checked I wonder. You did have the day off after all, but I keep both my thoughts and mouth to myself. Leaving them to it, I sprint back upstairs to check on the girls' homework and what's for dinner.

"Rosie, what smells so good in here?" Rosie has the range loaded with pots and the oven on 350!" "Hello Mrs. M, how was your day?" Rosie's an amazing chef! Keenan and I don't make requests for dinner anymore. We just allow Rosie the run of the kitchen. She ensures that we have a well-balanced diet but make no mistake, we're a soul food family!

Rosie came to be with us when I was eight months pregnant with the twins and has been my right-hand woman in the house since. Once we all became comfortable with one another, it was like she was a second mom rather than a "House Manager". Her family is from Puerto Rico and ten years after Rosie joined us, we invited her youngest sister, Natalia to come over and attend the University of Minnesota and assist Rosie as needed. Truth be told, Rosie does everything a housewife would do. Rosie doesn't want or need help from anyone including Natalia. With her unwavering loyalty to our family, bringing her sister over to attend college was the least Keenan and I could do for their family. We have a small guesthouse which was perfect for them both. Neither have kids so it made sense for all involved that they take the guesthouse versus commuting. "Rosie, can you let me know when dinner is ready," I ask. "Sure thing Mrs. M," she responds.

Before I can make my way upstairs and into the bedroom, I realize I've left my bags in the car. As I start sprinting back downstairs, here comes trusty Rosie with everything. "Rosie, you didn't have to go to the car, you're cooking!" She just smiles, shakes her head and continues past me and into the bedroom. "Mrs. M, I noticed the door was open leading to the garage and saw the bags through the window. Besides, that stove practically cooks the meals itself!" It took a few years to convince her, my kitchen was officially her kitchen. Hell, the only time I'm in there is when something smells good, or I need to speak with her concerning the kids or our home.

Finally, back in my bedroom! Time for these Louboutin's to come off. Don't let anyone tell you differently, expensive boots and shoes can be just as painful on a sistah's feet as a Wal-Mart or Target brand if not worse! "Name brand my ass," I wince while removing them. They are not all they're cracked up to be! It's time to run a nice bubble bath with "Midnight Pomegranate" salts. "Keenan," I text, "I have something special for you after dinner!" I include a selfie wearing nothing but my birthday suit before sliding into a warm bubble bath. My philosophy is the way you get the man is the way you must keep the man! For the most part, I try to keep that mindset knowing his libido is always in overdrive up until late, that is.

This bath is incredible! If you don't get an orgasm in a whirlpool bath, you're dead! The jets surrounding my garden tub and on bottom can make you lose yourself for hours. Unfortunately, I don't have that kind of time tonight!

As I relax and allow the jets to massage my body, all I can do is think about Ronald. What the hell is wrong with me? My lust for a man other than my husband has never been this out of control! Is it true once a woman turns forty and is keenly aware of what she enjoys sexually, her drive intensifies? Whatever the case, my drive is on overload, and I need my husband to get back with the program! The problem is, I'm not thinking about my husband right now. I'm going back to the daydream I had of Ron earlier. "I wonder if Ron's an ass man", I ponder aloud while laughing to myself. I know Keenan is and I must admit, I like it just as much as my husband does.

Rosie knocks on the door. "Dinner is almost done Mrs. M." "Great! Thanks Rosie, I'll be down in a couple of minutes," I respond. I hurry out of the bath and slip on a tank and sweats to have dinner with the family.

Rosie prepared baked salmon, pilau rice, steamed asparagus, garlic breadsticks with an arugula salad and balsamic vinaigrette. It's important that we sit down as a family for dinner at least twice a week. The twins normally are in track and field this time of year but due to the Pandemic, sports have been canceled throughout the school district. Sunday dinners are a different story and a must in my eyes! If Keenan isn't out of town on business, we make a big deal of it. Victoria is always here with us along with Justin and his wife though I'm on the verge of telling him to leave that bitch at home or don't come but I digress!

After dinner, we all gather in the family room to watch "The Hate You Give". I've watched it more than once, but Keenan doesn't know that. The movie is just over two hours long, so the kids still have more than enough time for a bath before bed. Being that my children attend a predominately white school, this movie really does hit home, this could very well be a reality for my children, something that weighs heavily on my mind. Halfway through the movie, Kee falls asleep. Instead of waking him up, I usher my children upstairs for baths followed by bedtime. I allow my husband to rest as I slip into something raunchy!

Keenan's favorite color is royal blue. The intimate wear Jackie picked for me is a laced, full body, one-piece with openings in the crotch and anal area. It comes complete with thigh high 5" stilettos, 8" gel dildo with rotating pearls, 4" inch ass beads and a 16" whip (cause I love a good spanking), and one hundred percent human lace front blue and black wig to complete the look, no jewelry necessary. I let go of the matching costume jewelry a long time ago when Keenan kept breaking my shit!

"Why are you not upstairs taking care of your Wifey," I ask with a slight irritation in my voice. "Coming up now love!" Showtime! I light a few candles and turn on Pandora to 90's R &B station. It's one of only a few stations that continue to keep R. Kelly in their rotation. I know a lot of folks want his black ass in jail for life right now and if everything on that Lifetime documentary was, true he absolutely deserves it! However, as a lawyer, he's innocent until proven guilty. And one more tidbit, where the fuck we're all the parents?! I mean, was it okay for the girls to go cause the money was good and now that it's not, there's a problem? I would never allow my children to be alone with any man or woman no matter how huge a superstar! I don't think any responsible parent would, but others have no qualms pimping their children for a perceived come up! Add to the fact that he went on trial for raping a young girl previously also didn't seem to matter to the parents. The fact Kelly actually married a very young teenage Aaliyah? How many red flags does one need? That has and never will make sense to me! My honest opinion, the parents, his handlers and everyone who condoned, enabled and encouraged his behavior should also be on trial! And for all the stars who came out to "mute R Kelly", probably half still listens to his music when no one's watching, just a little food for thought. Anyway, I run to the bathroom to give myself a once over. Before I can make it back to the bedroom, he's already banging on the door.

"MyeZelle," he barks, "where you at baby?" Knock, knock, knock, I respond from the other side of the bathroom door. "Oh, okay baby, I got you! Yeah, who's there," as he opens the door. "Your wife said she couldn't be with you tonight and sent me instead," I reply in a soft and sultry whisper. "Damn baby, who are you and wherever

18

my wife at, call her and tell her to stay her ass right there!" I'm almost offended but we are role playing after all. Instead, I push him aside, walk towards the bed, shaking what my momma gave me while rubbing my breasts. I climb on the bed and usher him over. "So. daddy, what would you like to do?" Keenan's looking as if I am truly someone else. "Baby, do you have a blonde wig," he asks. Are you fucking kidding me?!

I'm the perfect bedroom freak any man would want and my husband, my man is asking me for a fucking blonde wig?! And he wonders why I call his ass "half black"! I don't allow that to deter me, get your ass on your knees and do something to make me feel better is all I'm thinking about right now! I disregard what he just said, "no baby, I don't have a blonde wig, what I do have is a fat, juicy, wet-ass pussy in your face, now bow down," as I spank him playfully with my feathered whip.

Now I'm getting the response I'm used to! "Yeah, what's your name?" I think for a split second, "Becky with the good hair," that thought quickly leaves my mind. Keenan has a little too much "Tom" in him as it is! I chuckle a bit out loud and say, "you can call me Sunny baby."

After a brief stint of dirty talking, honey gets down to business. I must say, when we are on the same accord, our intimacy level is all the way up, a hundred out of a hundred. Keenan doesn't disappoint! He caresses, massages and kisses every inch of my body that's in need. We take our time and enjoy one another for a couple hours before tapping out. After a quick shower together, we drag ourselves to bed, quickly falling asleep in each other's arms. It was a great night!

✎ **Keenan**

DAMN, I DIDN'T REALIZE MY BABY WAS GONNA PUT IT down like that last night, shit! I mean, I love my sweetheart and all, she my girl, my lover, my friend and my wife. I don't know what the hell is wrong with me! Am I a sex addict, I'm not sure? The woman gives me everything I need, but man, new pussy is just something I crave! Now my sweetheart gave me four kids, the first two are double mini me's! And my little princess', they are my angels! Beautiful, just like their Mom! You know, we have this great life, I don't understand why I go out on my wife and fuck around, I just do!

Maybe it's the one thing I don't like about my wife, she's just too fucking real! I'm a real brother but she takes the shit to a whole other level. I didn't forget where I came from and even if I wanted to, she reminds me of the shit every other day! Yeah, I hang around brothers of another color. I learned a lesson a long time ago, in order to get ahead and stay ahead, you must diversify your portfolio and your friends! So yeah, I mingle with the pale skin brothers but I'm making that long money, right?!

MyeZelle seems to forget that I was raised on the west side of Chicago just as she was. I grew up around gangstas, pimps, hoes and poverty. I had to fight throughout my childhood. I made it to my high school graduation without being shot, stabbed or robbed. I knew if I could escape that, college and success thereafter would be a piece of cake!

So yeah, do I mingle with anyone and everyone who can elevate me even further, absolutely, I get the bag! You know, I guess that's just one of the reasons why my wife and I are having some issues.

Once I was able to get out, I didn't fucking look back! I'm not one of them brothers that go back to the hood and try to build up the community, the community didn't do a damn thing for my family back then, so I don't give a Chicago rat's ass about it now! My wife, however, takes time off every summer to go back to Chicago for some initiative bullshit, "Black Girls Move" program to help girls in the old neighborhood. They sign contracts in middle school to be the "best they can be" and if they graduate high school, they get scholarships for college. I can't lie, she raises a lot of money each year for her little pet project and 98% of the girls who sign the contract follow through and actually get into great colleges and graduate. By that same token, MyeZelle could be spending that time focusing on our family and businesses! If my wife did everything I wanted her to, I probably wouldn't be such an asshole and a skirt chaser!

✑ The Deal is Done

"AYE KEE, GET OVER HERE AND MEET THE LADIES!" WE are celebrating a closing tonight on a building downtown. It's small but it's going to put a couple million in my and my boy's pocket so it's a win. I walk up and as usual, its bitches everywhere! Blondes, red-heads, brunettes, you name it, they in here! The only thing they have in common is, they will do anything just to be in your space! I guess you can call them groupies for the elite businessmen of Minneapolis. We're always VIP in the hottest spots around the Twin Cities and the women are always there! We don't give them money like the rappers and athletes, at least I don't. Now my boy,

Justin, he throws money their way like we're at a damn strip club! It's crazy that some women will see men and they just smell the money. They're not looking for love, husband or a family, they just want to have a good time for however long the party lasts. Hell no, they want fifteen minutes of fame on their damn instagram or twitter accounts. Some of these THOTS know I'm married with kids, and they still don't give a damn! I suppose sitting in VIP, getting wasted and possibly screwed on a Friday or Saturday night and posting pictures is more than enough for these hoes!

Whenever Justin and I acquire a new contract or close a deal, we celebrate just like this!

I'm a sucker for a white broad, I can't even lie! They're just very different from black women, a complete 180! You can ask them for anything, and they'll do that shit! You know sexually, they up for any and everything! It's nothing you can't ask that they won't do 99% of the time. After fucking them, you can tell them to go cook a full course meal or a sandwich and chips at four o'clock in the morning, without hesitation or mouthy bullshit, they do it, no questions asked, just, "sure babe!"

I have a special one that I've been seeing for over three years. I take care of her because she knows the rules and well, she's special. Lindsey understands she's the side piece and is fine with that. She's never allowed in the same establishment I'm in unless I've already given her permission ahead of time. She's not allowed to call or text me after five no matter what! If I happen to take the day off, I give her a heads up to not contact me. If I want her, I'll call her! Most importantly, don't ever mention me on social media in any shape, form or fashion! I showed her pictures of my wife and children one day just to make a point. That point was, "if I ever fuck with you, don't ever think you'll replace my family," she understood, accepted all the rules and we've been good since. I did have to cut her ass loose for a while last year when she "accidentally" got pregnant. I forced her to get an abortion and have her tubes tied. Once she assured me the surgery was taken care of, I gave her a second chance. I never put a "glove" on it and had to take some part of the blame, so I gave her a second chance, I mean I am a nice guy, you know what I mean!

"What up J?" Justin is definitely my brother from another mother! "Man G, we got our girls here, titties, pussy and ass everywhere," he boasts with a smile. We're sitting in VIP at Aqua Lounge, its only 7:30 in the evening and some of these broads are already white girl wasted! Getting one of them in bed or hell the private bathroom here is like shooting fish in a barrel as this point. I can't miss if I tried!

"Mando, where have you been?" I have yet to meet this broad but she bad as hell! Man, I haven't seen anything this fine in a minute! Gorgeous face, beautiful white smile, and titties got to be a 38-40 double D! She's got an ass as big as my wife and she's white but with a nice tan like them east coast Jersey broads, a total fucking package! "Damn sweetie can a brother get a drink before you push up on me," I respond, giving her the indication I have absolutely no interest. I'm playing a role cause I already know in my head, I'm about to be on some bullshit yet again but this sexy may be worth the bullshit!

Justin and I kick it up for a short time discussing the deal finalized today and the Shapiro meeting. "Man J, with this deal today and the potential Shapiro deal coming up, we will be set for life. After that brother, we will be working maybe forty hours a week if that, earning double what we are now!" "I'm with you Kee, all the way man, we've got a good life and shits about to blow all the way up brother, I'm so ready for this next level," Justin exclaims! After more discussion about the success of today and future plans, my attention turns back to this fine ass woman throwing the pussy at me!

"What's up Ma, what's your name and what's up with calling me Mando?" This broad is banging! She's not Rican or Cuban. She looks like she could be Armenian, like them Kardashian sisters. Now that I actually focus on her, she looks like a younger version of Kim Kardashian, more like that baby sister. You know young but definitely grown, hasn't fucked her looks up yet with all that plastic surgery bullshit women are into today! "I'm Aryah," she replies. As she stands, I promise, you can balance a glass of wine on that fat ass with no problem! "I called you Mando because I've heard some things about you Mando. I'm a friend of your friend, Lindsey, actually ex friend I should clarify," she responds. Well damn, my head spinning a little from what she just said or is it the liquor? What the fuck did this bitch just say to me aloud! I respond, "who the hell is Lindsey?!"

Whatever attraction I had for this bitch quickly vanishes along with the rise that was growing in my pants. "Who the fuck is Lindsey," I demand! "Lindsey is, was my best friend until I walked in on her and my husband in my bed just over a month ago." She goes on to explain that her and Lindsey grew up as childhood friends and continued to be besties throughout their school years but lost contact once they both went off to college. "I moved back to Minneapolis when my mom became ill, and we reconnected. We picked up right where we left off and three months ago, she stood as my Maid of Honor. Fast track to last month, I went out of town on a photo shoot and decided to come home early to surprise my husband. I walk in, drop my bags and run upstairs only to find that whore riding my husband's dick," she barks! Now I'm really spinning and it's not the alcohol!

Aryah continues with her rant noting how she pretended to forgive Lindsey and her husband but really didn't. She actually managed to steal Lindsey's phone, crack her password and thus find out her secret lover, me! "Let me make this clear to you sweetheart, I will handle Lindsey since you already know what it is but this revenge shit you're thinking about and putting me in the middle of is dead! Get the fuck outta my space and go get drunk with the rest of them hoes over there, I'm not checking for you!" I have to get out of here right now! I let Justin know I'm heading downstairs for some air and will be back. "When I get back J, I want these bitches gone, we need to talk."

Once I'm on the outside, I feel like l can breathe cause Aryah's confession felt like a gut punch! I hit Lindsey's line right away cause Aryah has a brother shook! "Hey Linds, what are you up to?" She goes on about her day, but I don't give a damn about none of that. "Listen," I say, "I'll be stopping by after I finish some things up with J." I don't give her a chance to respond before hanging up.

After a few more minutes of fresh air, I head back in to wrap things up with Justin before leaving to confront Lindsey's ass. I see J has dismissed most of the drunk groupies with the exception of Ms. Aryah and his 2-piece choice for the night. "Aye J, get the rest of these bitches outta here, I need to holla at you man!" The look on my face, Justin knows I mean business. "Ladies, we need some privacy. Go dance, powder your noses or whatever the fuck it is all y'all do together," he laughs!

After they leave the area, I hit Justin with the bullshit Aryah just fed me. "So J, do you know what this broad just told me?! She says she and Lindsey used to be best friends until she caught the bitch in her bed with her fucking husband!" The blood has completely drained from Justin's face. I continue, "Aryah says the shit just happened like a month ago. J, this bitch been fucking her best friend's husband. Not only is she fucking him, but she went to the broad's crib and screwed this cat in her best friend's bed," I yell! Justin takes a few minutes to let everything sink in I just hit him with. "Kee, I can see the hoe messing around on you, you're married but she betrayed her girl like that, damn that's some wicked shit!" We go back and forth a while longer before leaving the club, not bothering to link back up with the THOTS who thought they were gonna be put on tonight.

I have Justin follow me to Lindsey's condo because I'm feeling a little tipsy at this point. When we arrive, Justin immediately jumps out of his whip and runs over to my car in a panic! "Look Kee, on the real, don't go up there and do nothing stupid. This broad ain't worth what you got going on. Hell, you can have ten damn Lindseys! Man, you could have taken Aryah's ass to the spot tonight. The way she was throwing it, I would have knocked that out with no problem!" I listen because I know my brother is telling me the right thing, but I am pissed! "Justin I'm cool man, I'm gonna let this bitch know that I KNOW, and it's been one. Her fifteen minutes up J. I'm cool man, I'll get up with you tomorrow at the office!" Once I assure my boy that everything is cool, he takes off.

I let myself in and Lindsey is on the sofa with a glass of wine. I immediately jump to it. "So, what's up? What the hell you been up to", I ask in a stern voice. I'm trying to hide my anger and remember the conversation Justin and I had less than five minutes ago, but the rage is showing. "So, take a wild guess who introduced themselves to me tonight. I'll give you a hint, you know her." She's looking at me puzzled, but not saying a word. "Tell you what, think about it while you fix me a drink," I demand. Lindsey brings me a double shot of Hennessey and hits me with the "sweet, valley girl bullshit". "Keenan, I have no idea who you're talking about, where have you been? I miss you; I haven't seen you in like four days," she exclaimed!

She slides on the sofa next to me and starts kissing my neck and rubbing on me as if I'm the best thing she's seen since sliced bread. I hit her with the shit, "do me a favor, grab your phone and bring it to me right now." Lindsey appears to be shaken and slightly confused but I don't budge. "Give me your phone, unlocked, I'm not fucking around, right now!" She walks to the island in the kitchen, picks up her phone and begins to shake. For a split second, I felt the fear in Lindsey, but it quickly dissipates. I walk over and snatch the phone, "let me get that!" As I walk back to the sofa I immediately start scrolling through her phone while holding mine. Aryah's number is third on the contact list and I instantly punch her number into my phone, cause yeah, I'm calling her! I get that and move on to the text messages. I want to see who this bitch been commuting with on any DM's, texts, videos and whatever else is out there. I check the texts first, followed up with all her social media shit. There are a few dudes' names that keep popping up but one is everywhere. This broad has been sending pictures, videos, and he's sent the same in return. I grill her ass about who this "Randell" guy is and between the hysterics and crocodile tears, I'm over it! "Lindsey, I want to know what's going on with you and this guy and don't you fucking lie to me! Your girlfriend told me everything. You're fucking another woman's husband in their house yet you're telling me I'm the only one!"

Through tears, Lindsey pleads her case but I'm not here for this bullshit. "I can't believe I actually trusted you. You're just like them white trash bitches I see in the clubs. I'm done with you, and I'll bring your phone back to you tomorrow after I make sure every trace of me has been removed from it!" "Kee, you cannot take my phone. I need it. What you're doing right now is a total invasion of my privacy! I don't understand how you can be so high on your horse when you're married! You don't spend time with me the way you used to, yet you expect me to just sit around and wait for you! I killed my baby so that I could be with you, what more do you want from me Keenan!" "Lindsey that sob story don't work on me! You knew what you were getting into when you met me. You knew the rules and you broke them so now I have to punish you and when I decide just how to do that, you'll be the first to know!" I know I have her shook and that's exactly the way I want her, off her square! "You have a landline, use it to call whoever you need to call. I'm sure your ass got a little black book somewhere. Hoes like you always got a backup plan. I'll be back tomorrow after I hit the office." With that, I walk out.

I'm damn near sober at this point. All this drama, hell and I have yet to make it home. I'm pissed at Lindsey, but I should have known not to trust her ass after she "accidentally" became pregnant. I put Lindsey out of my mind for the moment to focus on something else. I call Ms. Aryah, "Hey what's up this Mando." There's a long pause before she responds. "Hi, how are you? How did you get my number as I don't recall giving it to you after being brushed off tonight?" She sounds hurt but I don't give a shit either way. "Yeah, my bad lil mama, it was a lot going on this evening. But ugh yeah, so what are you up to?" I'm already knowing that she's not doing shit cause her husband is still in the doghouse! "Well, I'm not doing anything really, home having a glass of wine and relaxing, what's up?" I let her know I want to see her this weekend. I'm the kind of guy who always has a master plan and with Lindsey, I plan on pulling her hoe card and using Aryah to assist me. After spitting a little game to Aryah, I convince her to hook up Saturday night. Now it's time to go home and deal with MyeZelle's ass. By the time I make it home it's 3:00 in the morning.

My wife is up when I get home and she is pissed about something. "What's up baby," asking as if I don't already know what it is. "The question is what's up with you Mr. Washington. You drag your raggedy ass in here at 3:00 in the morning on a weekday, don't answer your phone or texts and you're asking me what's up? What's up with you?!" Damn, I've been dealing with bullshit all night and now I have to come home to some more?! Instead of getting angry, I apologize and lie. MyeZelle comes around after a few minutes of me groveling. Now that that's out of the way, I undress and crawl into bed next to my queen. I may have fallen asleep before my head hit the damn pillow.

ℰ Victoria

I LOVE MY GIRL LIKE I LOVE FRESH AIR. SHE'S LIKE MY left side. We know everything about each other. One of my girl's flaws is, MyeZelle loves to be loved. It's not a want for her, it's a need, a must. I'm a bit more than concerned about this situation she has going on with her client, Ronald Henderson. I get that Keenan is a cheating asshole and he's not giving her everything she needs so I totally understand that, and I sympathize. Hell, I've been by her side throughout her husband's cheating scandals and I know she's getting to the point where she's ready for a little revenge! Mr. Henderson is a very attractive and well put together brother, I get the attraction. I'm hoping by taking him on as a client will stop this lust train before it ever leaves the station.

After speaking with MyeZelle, I prepare to head home, it's been a long day. Thank GOD my home is a short drive from the office because I need a drink!

I never had kids so I'm godmother to Keenan and MyeZelle's children. I actually get the best of both worlds. The kids come over on weekends when Mye and Kee need a getaway, or she travels with him for business. I bought a three-bedroom condo so that I have space for them GOD forbid something was to ever happen. I'm an animal lover, they require a little less attention and don't talk back. I have a 250-gallon saltwater aquarium in my sitting room filled with clown, lion and coral reef fish. I'm also a huge dog lover. My babies are pure American Staffordshire terriors, Shaka and Zulu. They're very family friendly and really gentle with my godchildren but are fiercely protective.

"Hey MyeZelle, did you get in touch with Ronald," I ask. After a brief pause, Mye explains that she hasn't called Mr. Henderson. "I'm sorry girl, I had some errands to run once I left the office and totally forgot. I will give him a call now. Give it about thirty minutes and you can go ahead and make the call to him." I sigh, "so how upset do you think he's going to be about this change," I ask. We go back and forth for a bit discussing why the change is necessary and I can't come up with a valid reason for the change. "MyeZelle, you need to be honest with this man. I don't see him taking this well. After you call him, give me a call back and let me know what's up." She agrees to give Ronald a call and with that taken care of, I hang up.

I pour myself a glass a wine and exit left for my patio. Its cool outside but I can use the fresh air. This is one of those days where I wish I had someone to come home to and help me decompress. I've been single for over two years now. MyeZelle always says that I'm very picky, but I just feel like I haven't met anyone that completes me. I made a profile on a couple dating sites, Match and E Harmony. I've had some really good dates but there was always something not quite right with the guy. He's either too thin or not tall enough. His hands and or feet are too small. It sounds silly to have those sort of hang ups and dismiss a guy simply because his shoe size isn't a 12 or larger but there are certain qualifications I must have in a man! He must have nice brown skin or darker and at least 6' 2". He must have a beautiful pearly white smile and yes, big hands and large feet! He must be financially stable, and career driven with no children. I don't have the time nor energy for anyone's "baby momma" drama. Whenever you go into a relationship with a man with children, best believe, the bitches he has children with are going to feel some type of way no matter how long they've been apart. With all that I require for a man, it's been extremely difficult to say the least. I haven't completely given up on love, I'm just praying God will bring him soon because I'm not getting any younger.

There was one guy I thought could be the one. Gary is a former NBA player and now owns "Sanctuary", a very successful restaurant downtown. This guy was perfect. He's 6' 9" with large hands and large feet and everything else large if you know what I mean. His skin is a smooth cocoa brown with hazel eyes and a perfect smile. The sex was absolutely amazing, everything was perfect! I'm not exactly sure what went wrong. We went on several dates and things seemed to be going well and then nothing. I called a couple times after our last date and got no response, so I let it go. I chalked it up to the NBA lifestyle. Though he's retired, he has yet to marry or have children, so I just figure he has some more playing to do.

My phone rings and its MyeZelle. "Hey Vic, it's me. You can call Ron, but I think it's just going to be a waste of time. He's refusing to allow the switch. I don't know what to do to get this man out of my damn life!" I listen and I sympathize but I'm not so sure she really wants him out of her "damn life" as she puts it. "Mye, I don't know what to tell you. I mean, if you go before the judge and ask to be recused, the judge is going to ask you why. I mean, what are you going to say, your Honor, my client makes me horny. You're Honor, I can no longer represent Mr. Henderson due to my pussy catching fire and throbbing every time I lay eyes on him," I laugh. She joins in on the laughter but we both know this is not a laughing matter. "Mye, I'm still going to give him a call before he has time to think about it. Maybe I can convince him it's for the best. Don't worry girl, all he can do is tell me no as well. I'll see you in the morning and don't stress yourself, everything is going to be fine." I end the call and grab another glass of wine before calling "Mr. Sexy Man".

I dial Mr. Henderson's number and shock, shock, it goes to voicemail. "Hi Ronald, this is Victoria Porter, MyZelle Washington's law partner. I would like to set up a meeting with you tomorrow at 10am, my office if possible. Please return my call to confirm, thank you Mr. Henderson." I don't expect him to call back, but I can say that I tried.

I take a hot bath and get ready to watch Lifetime. Just as I crawl into bed, my phone rings. It's a private number so I let it go to voicemail. A couple minutes later, again my phone rings and on the other end is a private call. This time I answer, "this is Victoria Porter." "Ms. Porter, this is Ron Henderson, I got your voicemail." I'm shocked, one that he bothered to call back, two that he's so polite. I guess I was expecting a thug on the other end. "Yes, how are you Mr. Henderson," I ask nervously. "I'm good. Listen I don't know how much you know about my case or my relationship with MyeZelle, I mean Mrs. Washington but I'm not changing lawyers so I really don't think it will be necessary for the two of us to meet." I sigh, "look Mr. Henderson, Mrs. Washington is my business partner and I trust her judgment. There has to be a valid reason why she would want to recuse herself. Can we just set up a meeting and go over your case together? If at that point, you still feel my partner must remain on your case, that's something the two of you will have to work out." He responds, "I'm really busy during the week and I'm sure you don't do business meetings on the weekend, so I don't see this happening," Ronald responds. If this prick thinks that will force me to drop this, he's got another thing coming. "That's not a problem Mr. Henderson, how is Saturday, say about 11AM?" Ronald finally agrees to the meeting, and we bid each other a goodnight. I think to myself, maybe this will work out after all. After sending MyeZelle a text informing her of the good news, I return to my Lifetime movie before finally falling asleep.

The rest of the week goes by smoothly and Saturday rolls around. I make it to the office by 9AM after dropping by Panera to pick up breakfast for Mr. Henderson and myself. I also need to get an early jump on a few cases I have on the books for court on Monday. Time seems to fly by and before I know it, its 11:45 and Mr. Henderson is nowhere to be found and I'm a little more than pissed! I try Ronald's number several times only to get his voicemail. I send a text and still nothing, now I'm livid.

"What's up chic," I question MyeZelle in a very agitated tone. I hear nothing but crickets, she knows I'm upset! "Mr. Henderson never showed this morning!" I could tell by Mye's long sigh she wasn't surprised in the least. "Damn it, I knew this would happen! Did he at least call to reschedule," she responds in a soft whisper. "Have you checked your voicemail for the office and your cell, e-mail?" She's really trying my patience at this point. "Mye, I'm in the office! I've been in the office since 9 this morning, on a Saturday no less just to meet Mr. Henderson. So no, he hasn't left me any messages and I never gave him my e-mail address. What is really going on with you and this guy?" I know she's got it bad for the guy, shit it's easy to understand why, the brother fine as hell! Being her best friend, I also know that this is a disaster waiting to happen. "Vic, meet me for an early dinner so we can talk. Bar La Grassa, 5:30. Will that give you enough time?" I agree on dinner with MyeZelle and we end the call. I wrap up the paperwork remaining on my desk, lock up the office and head home.

I'm rushing through the door as my cell phone continuously rings. After throwing my briefcase and purse on the kitchen island, I finally check my phone and I can't fucking believe it, it's a blast from the past, Gary's ass! Before I can collect my thoughts, he calls again and this time I answer, quickly. "This is Victoria Porter," I answer, as always. "Hey, what's up love," he asks. We haven't spoken in over two months so I'm wondering why he's decided to call now. I respond, "hey what's going on?" We make small talk for a short time before he gets into the bullshit excuses of why he went "ghost".

Gary attempts to justify his absence by saying he felt like he was falling for me too quickly and when I made it clear that I wasn't looking for anything serious, he decided to back off. He apologizes profusely but I'm not moved. "Gary, I'm not sure what to say right now. I mean, I want to understand but a return phone call explaining just the way you did now would have helped a couple of months ago. I accept your apology and wish you well as always," attempting to hang up. "Victoria, please wait baby, don't hang up. Will you have dinner with me tonight, please?" While he's groveling, my first thought is to gut punch his ass and say, "thanks but no thanks". "Victoria, at least let me buy you dinner and apologize in person. It's just dinner, I'll be on my best behavior, I promise baby." After letting him sweat a few moments longer, I agree to meet at his restaurant at 8 tonight. "I'll be there but I'm having a business dinner at 5:30 with MyeZelle so chances are I won't be very hungry." "Sweetheart, can you cancel with MyeZelle,

I want to make you something special. Is there any way you can get out of it?" I think about it for a moment and agree to blow Mye off. After all, I did waste time on her asshole client today, more than that, I believe my best friend hasn't been completely forthcoming with the Mr. Henderson saga anyway. After more small talk I end the call with Gary and give MyeZelle a call.

"Hey Mye, I have to cancel dinner tonight." "Why, what's going on," she responds. "I'm actually having dinner with Gary tonight." She seems stunned. "Why would you give that asshole the time of day," she demands and proceeds to go on a rant. "How long has it been since you've spoken to him? Not only that, where the hell has he been and what excuse did he come up with as to why he disappeared?!" I give her the short version of Gary's excuses. "Vic don't buy the bullshit he's trying to sell you girl! He is playing you! He was probably screwing some white bitch, got bored and now he wants his brown sugar back. Don't fall for it!" I love my girl, but she can really irritate my whole soul at times. Before I can stop myself, I respond very nastily! "Mye, all black men don't want a skinny ass white girl, that's your husband's kryptonite sweetie! And as far as that goes, since when did you become a freaking racist? Just because Keenan screws white whores doesn't make all white women bad, for GOD sake's MyeZelle!" I immediately feel like shit for saying that to my girl. "I'm sorry Mye, I didn't mean to hit below the belt like that, I'm just wound up. Look, I was out of line and I sincerely apologize. I just don't want you to look at the world so black and white because of Keenan's actions. Being a proud black woman doesn't mean every white woman is your enemy Sis, just the ones who have no respect for your family or themselves." "It's all good Vic, and no you didn't have to say that bullshit and yes, we both know exactly what type of asshole I'm married to but anyway. And with everything going on in the country right now that's the last perception I would want anyone to think of me, the shit just hurts, you know?! I'll let you go so that you can relax before your date." "Do you forgive me Mye," I ask concerned. She responds yes and I ask if she will come over to help me get ready for my date and of course my best friend agrees.

I've barely gone through my closet before my phone starts ringing back-to-back, and of course its MyeZelle calling hysterical. "Mye, what's going on, are you not coming," I ask. Yes, I'm coming, and you won't believe this, Ronald Henderson is following me right now," she screams! Oh my God, what is wrong with this guy, I think. "Mye, just come to me and if that idiot follows you here, I will use Ms. Nina on his ass!"

It took her almost 45 minutes to get here. In true stalker fashion, he really followed her to my home but drove on after he saw that I was downstairs waiting for MyeZelle. "Girl, get in here, I can't believe this ninja just pulled this shit!" MyeZelle looks terrified! It makes me wonder has she slept with this guy and too afraid or ashamed to tell me the truth.

After making our way into my condo, we just sit for what seemed like forever before MyeZelle breaks the silence. "I have no idea when he started following me! I look in my rearview and he's just there! I drove around downtown for a short time hoping he would just give up. I can't believe he followed me here!" MyeZelle continues, "Vic, I dream about this man, I've had fantasies about him, but I haven't slept with him. I've never touched him inappropriately, but he can feel the sexual tension as much as I can! I don't know what the attraction is but it's magnetic, it's like this man can read my thoughts. I don't know what I'm going to do. I don't think he's gonna stop. Hell, I don't know if I want him to stop, honestly. Keenan is being Keenan. Maybe that's why I'm feeling this way about Ron or maybe it's because his ass is just so damn fine!" Now, back in the day, I would tell my girl to go for it. I mean, I love Kee, but he is a straight trick! He is the reason the word fucking exists! The man will fuck a manhole if it was shaped like a pussy! But this Ron is already a problem and if she gives him the goods, it's going to be some real shit and not just a fly by night sort of thing. If he's crazy enough to follow her to my house, what the hell else is he capable of? If they haven't sucked or fucked and he's already stalking, what is he going to do when Mye throws that shit on him, and I know how my best friend gets down!

"Mye look, you have to call him right now, let dude know that this shit is not cool, and he has to stop, this can get really ugly really fast. If you want, I will call him but it needs to come from you. You need to be stern and let his ass know in no uncertain terms to back off and mean it! Is he fucking stalking your house, does he know where you live?" MyeZelle continues to remain silent as I continue my rant. "If you don't stop this now and you go ahead and sleep with this crazy ass guy, you're going to open up a whole can of worms that could cost you a lot more than a wet ass! I'm serious Mye, get this guy out of your life now while you can." I can tell my girl is not listening to anything I've just said. She hears me but she is not listening!

I spend the next hour begging and pleading for her to stop this nonsense. I mean, damn, she hasn't touched the guy yet. I can only imagine what he's capable of if she ever does find herself in bed with him. I fix MyeZelle a drink and after a while, she calms down, and we discuss ways for her to get Ronald out of her life.

Now that she's gotten her composure back, Mye makes the very needed phone call to Mr. Henderson. "Ron, this is MyeZelle, listen our business relationship is over. I will refer you to a new law firm but as of this moment, you are no longer my client. I will be filing paperwork on Monday morning to recuse myself from your case." After a long pause, he responds, "MyeZelle just meet me for one drink, I really need to see you. Just to say goodbye, I don't want to leave it this way. I'm sorry I followed you. I just want you so bad, but I can respect your decision, just please meet me. I don't want you to think I'm this crazy nigga cause I'm not. You know my life story, I'm a good guy. You're just a woman I find irresistible, but I can respect your decision." "Mr. Henderson, I don't think that's a good idea, you really frightened me. It's not normal to follow someone like that!" "I'm not gonna stop until you at least meet me face to face. Just let me talk to face to face, away from your office and the courthouse, I'll leave you alone after that, I promise. I would never hurt you. I have the highest respect for you, and I was dead ass wrong to scare you. Please meet me MyeZelle." "Yes, Ron, that will be fine, text me the information." MyeZelle hangs up the phone and says, "he's okay with me dropping him as a client, everything is cool Vic." I know this girl didn't just look me in my eyes and lie to me!

She is really trying to feed me a platter of bullshit right now and I'm just not here for it! "MyeZelle, you are going to get burned fucking with this guy, leave his ass alone!" I can't say anything else. My girl is going to do exactly what she wants to do. All I can do is pray that I'm wrong and help her pick up the pieces that I know are about to start breaking. At this point, I change the subject, I'm over this!

"Alright girl, help me get ready for tonight. This should take your mind off "Stalker Boy", at least for a little while," I chuckle. We spend some time going through my wardrobe and I finally decide on an Alexander McQueen oversized bomber with matching mini dress, along with calf high leather boots. "Alright Missy, I think you have everything you need for tonight," MyeZelle quips. "You're sure right. I'm good to go now, thanks for helping girl," I laugh.

MyeZelle leaves and I get back to the business at hand, getting ready for my date with Mr. Gary.

I'm running a little late for dinner, fashionably late of course. I figure if he can make me wait over two months to call and apologize, he can wait another half hour for me to arrive for dinner!

After entering the restaurant, I immediately notice there's absolutely no one here! The hostess sashays over and directs me to the back of the restaurant where I spot Gary standing at a table for two. The lights are dim, candles and roses are everywhere! He has this huge smile on his face as if he's just won the freaking lottery, I can't take it, smiling to myself!

"How are you Victoria," he says while giving me the tightest, warmest hug and kiss on the cheek. "I'm fine thank you, how are you," I respond. He pulls out my chair and instead of taking a seat across the table, he sits right next to me. "I want to be close to you, I miss you Vic." I respond with a smile and nothing more. Gary again goes over the reasons why he pulled away. Looking into his eyes as he's pouring his heart out, I hate to admit it, but I believe him. "Well, I do understand to a point. I wish you would have been honest back then. That being sad, I do forgive you, its water under the bridge now for me."

Gary has really outdone himself with dinner tonight. We dine on steak and lobster along with a salad and very expensive bottle of wine. The night is going great, and we catch up on what's going on in each other's lives. I'm enjoying the dinner and the conversation, but it's been a very long day and I'm ready to call it a night, it's already after 11.

"Dinner was great, and the company was okay," I laugh, "but I have to get home." Gary tries convincing me to have a night cap but I'm not budging! "Just come back to my place, I will be a perfect gentleman, I promise Vic. I just don't want this night to end yet." Hell no, I'm not going back to your home, and you are not getting my sweet treats I think to myself! "I'm not going to your home and you're not coming back to mine, it's a no," I respond. Gary walks me out my car, gives me a kiss on the cheek and neck and we say goodnight. As I'm driving away, I laugh and think to myself, "damn girl, you could have gotten your back blown out tonight," oh well!

Finally, back home! It literally takes me under sixty seconds to undress and dive into bed. I don't bother to turn on the tv, goodnight to me!

◌ Ronald

I CAN'T LET THIS WOMAN GET AWAY FROM ME. I'VE BEEN looking for someone like her ever since I got my shit together. Man, all a good nigga from the hood wants is a beautiful, intelligent, fine ass woman on his side that's down! And I know she's a freak, I can tell by the way she walks. Man, it's like she has a runway in front her no matter where she is. It's a switch but she's not trying to switch, it's her natural walk and that ass just bounces from side to side, it's mesmerizing, hypnotic. You just know when you see a woman that has all that, she's a boss bitch. The only issue that makes me pause is the fact that she's married. Having four kids doesn't bother me in the least, hell I practically raised my younger sister and brother at a time when my aunt was struggling but we're good now.

The road to the good life wasn't quick or painless. My first hustle was as a "lookout". You know, make sure the guys working the blocks knew when "one time or 12" were rolling through. That bullshit didn't last long though; I wasn't making enough to feed my family. I moved up to dealing whatever I could get my hands on. You name it, I had it. I would sell anything; pills, weed, crack, heroin, meth, fentanyl, I mean anything! Don't get me wrong, I've always had a hang up dealing that bad shit, but junkies don't give a damn where or who they get their fix from so it may as well have been me! As I got older and stronger, I would muscle other hustlers out of their shit and sell it. The one time I was busted for drugs and got off easy, I knew I had to come up with a different plan. I damn sure wasn't going to leave my sister and brother alone with my aunt. As soon as I was old enough, I started bouncing for high end bars and strip clubs. I kept my street hustle going while I stacked my money.

Within a couple of years, I had my paper together. That's when I decided to go legit, mostly. I bought a couple bars that had been closed in the hood, fix them up and started making real good money. From there, I bought my first strip club downtown and then a second one. My first business venture in the restaurant industry came a year ago. It's an upscale joint just down the street from Prince's shit, "First Ave". Growing up the way I had to, I had to make hustling my air. I breathe that shit and when I see a business opportunity that's legit, I make that shit happen!

I sent her a text but never received a response so it's time to give my future wifey a call, smiling to myself. "MyeZelle, its Ron, I guess you didn't get my text. Will you meet me at Lixx Lounge?"

I'm sure she's heard about the club but what she doesn't know is, I just bought it. See the dope game can only last so long and if you don't have any legit businesses, you're not gonna last! The Feds can't touch a brother like me though cause I don't get my hands dirty on shit anymore! A few brothers in the hood I still fuck with, I make shit happen for them while they get their money up to hopefully do what I'm doing now. "Yes Ron, I will be there in a half hour, one drink and were done. I have a family I have to get home to." Hell yeah, I got her ass now! All I needed was one shot to get her away from her office and her nosy ass partner Victoria and a fucking courthouse full of cops!

I make it to the club before MyeZelle arrives. Lixx Lounge has four levels to it. The first floor is basically a lounge where many customers gather after work for drinks and a bite to eat. It's not a full restaurant but the chef has a nice array of appetizers to keep the Monday through Friday happy hour crowd pleased. I have a DJ through the weekday to play an array of genres depending on the crowd. The second level is set up exactly like the first level but it's strictly jazz music with live bands performing Thursday through Sunday. The chef's menu is more customized for dinner crowd. The third level is R & B, hip hop crowd. There's a huge dance floor with some seating areas and four separate VIP lounges where you can order dinner from the jazz lounge or appetizers from the happy hour lounge. I didn't want a restaurant area on this floor cause niggas get a little extra turnt when you got Drake, Kendrik Lamar, Migos, Cardi, Thee Stallion, Bruno Mars and Silk Sonic that we book for appearances!

Now the fourth floor is strictly for the money makers! You actually have to be on a list to get on this floor or be well recognized. This is where you see many of the A-Listers around town just hanging out amongst each other. After a game, concert or some shit like that, they bring they're entourage here. This level is about 5,000 square feet and gives the money makers the ability to look down onto the third floor while the floor to ceiling retractable glass partitions allow them to either keep the noise from below out or enjoy the sounds and crowd below with the touch of a button.

My personal VIP is secluded, half a staircase above the celebrity VIP sections. It's equipped with surveillance covering every inch of my club. The phone system is set up so I can reach security on all floors along with other staff and dining areas. With a personal bar and private exit leading to a master suite, I never have to leave on those nights when I'm absolutely worn out.

My staff has taken care of everything I requested for tonight. Candles are everywhere and the smell of warm lavender fills the room. Red, pink and white roses add to the sweet aroma. Ace of Spades, Ciroc and white wine are chilled and ready. I've also let my chef know to be on standby for anything Ms. MyeZelle may want for dinner, if I can keep her sexy ass here long enough. MyeZelle let it slip some of her favorite foods, so I've made sure everything this woman likes to eat, or drink is ready. Nothing is too much for my baby girl or soon to be baby girl I should say. I'm rocking a cream linen Versace suit and a simple pair of loafers. I have no intention of mingling with the crowd tonight, so I want to keep it casual. MyeZelle is attracted to shit like that. She likes a man that knows how to dress down but still looks like he's about business. I know that clown ass nigga she married don't have that gangsta drip I got. Shit if it wasn't for her kids, I would have already bullied her husband to a divorce and been smashing that fine ass!

The VIP is just the start of the many surprises I have for this woman tonight. MyeZelle is lady and a lady must be pampered, spoiled, the center of attention and has her every need and desire met on a consistent basis. If you can do that, a woman will be yours forever. MyeZelle truly only knows the side of me that's been in the streets, the side I pay her to defend, and she's attracted to that shit! Most women want a nigga with a little rough side and if they say they don't, they fucking lying. Now, if I can show her my softer, family man side, I may have a real shot with this woman.

ᑫ MyeZelle

I can't believe I'm actually doing this. I promised my girl that I would leave this man alone. One drink won't hurt, right? I think I know what I'm doing. No, I know what I'm doing! My thoughts are all over the place. All I have to do is keep my game face, lawyer attitude and pussy in check and I will be fine! I'm walking into this bar, having one drink and my business with Mr. Henderson is done.

As I enter the lounge, I immediately feel the romantic ambiance of the room. I'm greeted by not one but two very beautiful hostesses, who seems to know exactly who I am. It's a bit scary, at the same time, very exciting. Ron picked a great spot. The scene is very relaxed. You have people drinking, some are seated and eating, and a few couples are dancing off in the distance. This is very nice if I must say so myself! This man must have spent a few stacks to have these women cater to one woman through the door! I'm sure he's in with the owner somehow. Either way, the extra attention is very flattering.

All the décor from the walls to the furnishings are on point. It has a very chill vibe. After a hard day, this is a place for a nice escape after the office day-to-day bullshit. I have to bring Vic back on a day when we need to let our hair down after a long day!

The ladies escort me a bit further into the club where this hulk of a man is waiting. The guy could be Micheal Clark Duncan's twin, body wise, he's huge! I thought Ronald was a big guy but damn! Come to think of it, he reminds me of Ron, they look alike. Maybe they're related. They definitely have fineness and fitness in common, smiling to myself.

"Are you MyeZelle," the gentleman asks. "Yes, and you are," I respond. He gives me a smile and just ushers me to where he wants me to go, gently placing his hand on the small of my back. We move past VIP, and I notice a couple of my clients, Timberwolves players who are enjoying the company of some beautiful young ladies, none of whom are their wives but I'm not here for business with any of them, so I keep it moving and pray they don't notice me.

We make our way to an oversized door that opens to a hallway with an elevator and suddenly my nerves get the better of me and I'm overcome immediately with a sense of panic. I freeze in fear and my legs won't move. Sensing my fear, the guy tries reassuring me, "It's okay MyeZelle, Ron is waiting for you. You're in safe hands, it's all good Ms. Lady." I remind myself that this is a club and there has to be security cameras that saw my ass walk in here! He wouldn't do anything crazy inside a club full of people, would he?

After entering this floor to ceiling mirrored elevator, we make it to the 4th floor and there is Ron waiting as the doors open. He's looking as if I'm his last meal. I'm staring at him the very same way. I want this man! It's against everything I stand for as a married woman and unethical as a lawyer but there's something about him that is magnetic. He greets me with a very soft kiss on my neck and on the forehead. You just don't do that to a woman, the neck means I want you. The forehead means, I love and adore you. As a woman, kisses like that send a surge through your body. I maintain my composure enough to allow him to walk me through yet another door and into this beautifully decorated and very secluded VIP room.

As we sit, I can't help but be in awe of this room, this place altogether. "This is really beautiful Ron. You really didn't have to do all of this just for us to have one drink." He laughs, "and what is all of this that you think I've done exactly?" I know he spent a lot of money to get the girls downstairs to wait for me not to mention get the "Hulk" to escort me to this area. "I'm just wondering why you would spend so much money to have a drink because that's all that this is going to be Ron, a drink." He smiles, "MyeZelle, I didn't have to spend a dime on this tonight, I did spend a hell of a lot to get this place the way I wanted though," giving me a slight grin. "So", you've added to your business portfolio," I ask. "Yeah sweetheart, I need long paper to take care of you and four kids." Before I can respond, Ron walks over to the bar to prepare some drinks. Good thing, because I'm sure my mouth was wide open for a brief moment. I truly am in awe of this man, not a good thing for me, Keenan or our marriage!

I totally understand why this man hustled, fought, scratched and scraped his way to where he is today. When you have limited options, you are left with very few choices, I get that shit. I commend the brother and applaud the strides he has made and how he continues to elevate himself! My husband seems to have forgotten that the struggle was real for the both of us and that it continues to this day! While I do love him, I have a lot of resentment toward Keenan for that very reason!

Ronald makes us a couple drinks and rejoins me on the loveseat. At this point, we've shared more than the one-drink maximum I promised myself. After a couple hours of serious conversation about life, love and everything in between, he completely changes the mood and makes me laugh, really laugh. "Come with me, I want to show you something." I quickly shoot him the "hell to no" look! Ron laughs and gently pulls me off the sofa. Holding my hand, we exit the VIP area and enter these mahogany French doors just past the elevator and inside there's a private bedroom. As he closes the doors behind us, I quickly turn to him, "Ron, this is really nice, but I have to get home." He ignores me and pulls my body tightly into his. He begins kissing me, very passionately and for a few seconds I resist but ultimately give in. The kiss felt as if it went on for minutes and by the time it was over, my knees were shaking. Ron felt my body crumbling and scooped me in his arms like I was a newborn baby. He places me on the bed with multicolor roses surrounding my body.

Ron wastes no time slowly undressing me. He starts by kissing my forehead, my lips, nape of my neck, slowly caressing my breasts. I'm already moaning, damn near dripping wet! His lips are so soft and warm. His hands are hot, almost feverish. His body is so sculpted, all muscle and his skin is smooth. My body is craving him, and he knows it. He's kissing my navel and going further down. His tongue skills are amazing! I can't control my first orgasm. I've never been kissed and sucked on my clit in this way. Its slow and methodical, Ron's taking his time to make sure I'm satisfied. He's drinking my juices up and I can't help but tell him how he's bringing out every emotion possible in me right now. "Ron, I need you so bad honey! Your tongue feels so fucking good baby!" I let out this scream I never knew I had inside me and begged this man to fuck me and to fuck me now! I have the biggest orgasm I've ever experienced! He stands and I see this massive anaconda dick staring straight at me. I sit up and try to pull him towards me, but he pushes me back on the bed. "Turn your ass around and get on your knees now," he commands! I do exactly as requested, and Ron wastes no time pushing ten thick inches of all his manhood into my wet throbbing pussy. I feel like a virgin all over again, it hurts so good! We make love for hours, every position imaginable. I don't think I've ever been this completely drained after a good night of love making. He holds me so tightly and the night slips away from me.

I slowly awaken to the sounds of my phone ringing. I reach to grab it and its Keenan. I let the call go to voicemail and notice that its 6:30 in the morning. I jump up as if my ass is on fire, grab my clothes and run for the bathroom. Ron quickly follows. "Baby, what's wrong," he asks. What's wrong, thinking to myself! "What's wrong? What's wrong is I just spent the fucking night out away from my family, with a client no less! I cannot do this with you! Look at what has happened, the first time we get together, I don't go home! It's over Ron. Don't call me, text me, come to my office ever again, I mean it!" I quickly dress and brush pass him. "MyeZelle, wait. Look I'm sorry, I'll never put you in this situation again but don't say its over. I didn't mean to keep you out all night, I'm sorry baby, I swear!" I'm not trying to hear anything. "Ron, just show me how to get the fuck out of here, now please," I demand!

I finally make it to my car and race to Vic's house. She's the only one who can cover my ass and get me out of this mess I created. I know Vic is probably still sleeping, thank God we have keys to each other's homes in case of emergencies. This is an emergency, level twelve!

As I enter, I can hear Victoria's phone off in the distance. I race towards her room and she's up. "Where in the world have you been MyeZelle!" Before I can answer, Vic continues. "Do you know how many missed calls and texts I have from your damn husband? You took your ass to see Ron didn't you," she demands! I give her all the tea from my night out and she shakes her head in ire and disgust. "Please tell me that you haven't responded to any calls or messages Vic," I plead. After a tongue lashing, cursing out, she admits that she's been ignoring Kee's calls and texts as well. Finally, we both calm down and figure what extraordinary lie I can come up with that Keenan will believe. I've never done anything like this before. Sure, I have slept over to Vic's on a couple occasions after an argument with Keenan in the past, but it was because he fucked up, not me! When it's happened, I've always answered the phone to curse his ass out more before finally not responding and crying in my best friend's arms.

I put on the best groggy, hangover voice on that I could muster. His phone goes straight to voicemail. I don't bother leaving a message. After taking a quick shower and borrowing a track suit and a pair of Jordan's from Vic, I race home. My emotions are so all over the place, I'm barely capable of making it home without causing a wreck. I'm angry at Ron, myself and Keenan. Had my husband been paying attention to his wife, I would have never been in the situation I find myself in now!

Keenan

Where the hell is my wife?! "Mye, you need to answer your phone, where the fuck are you? I'm worried to death, Vic hasn't heard from you, the kids are worried, you need to call me! No, you need to bring your ass home!" Just as I'm hanging up the phone for the final time, I hear the alarm beeping. She's home. I race down to the garage. I'm in a rage but afraid at the same time. Where the hell could she have been all night and why didn't she call, is she hurt? So many things are running through my mind as I open the door to the garage. She's just sitting in her car staring into space. I open the car door. "Mye, where the hell have you been all night?!" She just gives me this black stare. I know this bitch ain't been with no nigga! "Answer me damn it, now MyeZelle!" She gets out of the car and just brushes past me, rushes in the house and proceeds to go upstairs. "I know damn well you don't think you taking your ass up to our bedroom after laying in another nigga's bed all night!" She turns with a look of horror on her face, but it doesn't faze me one bit. She's not injured, there's nothing wrong with the car. If she wasn't in an accident, the only other explanation is, she was out with another man. "Keenan, I don't feel well, Vic and I had too many glasses of wine and I fell asleep. I'm sorry, I should have called. Vic is going through some things, and I lost track of the time. I apologize for making you worry." I know she don't think I'm buying this weak ass line! My wife is very talkative when she drinks so her not answering the phone just doesn't make sense.

"I called Vic and she said she hadn't seen you since you left the office so stop fucking lying to me!" "Keenan, when Vic and I woke up, we had the same amount of calls on our phones from you. Vic didn't answer her phone and if she had, she would have gotten me up so don't lie! I'm sorry I stayed out, would you rather I got in my car and drove drunk," MyeZelle answers sharply.

Women can come up with a quick lie that's actually believable! "Don't give me that shit, I went by Victoria's last night and I didn't see your damn car anywhere so where we're you?" I can't wait for this comeback! "Keenan, I have a pass to the garage just like I have a key to the front door. Since when do I park my car on the street at Vic's if I'm there for a period of time? I'm sorry baby, but that's all that happened. Nothing else is going on, nothing Kee! All you had to do was ask the doorman to call upstairs, damn!" I don't believe a word she's saying but I don't have proof of anything else at least right now. "This shit better not happen again I know that!" I let it go cause MyeZelle is sticking to her story, but my gut is telling me that she's lying or maybe it's the fact that all my philandering has me paranoid.

"Justin, what's up man?" I know my white brother from another mother can help me figure this out! "What's up Kee?" I explain about Mye not coming home last night and I need his help. Justin will do anything for me as I will for him. I know she doesn't think I'm just gonna let that shit ride. If MyeZelle is doing anything, I will know soon enough! "Can you get away this afternoon," I ask. Of course, he can, Justin does whatever Justin wants! "Yeah man, no plans other than the games, what's going on?" "I'll explain everything when we link up, I'll call you this afternoon." I don't give him time to answer before hanging up.

I know I'm doing some fucked up things when it comes to my marriage but I'm a man! I've always known that I could depend on MyeZelle to do certain things without fail. She's a brilliant attorney, takes care of home, our kids, handles the finances and has never gone outside our marriage that I'm aware of. The thought that she may have cheated has my mind all over the place. I've always had complete control of my household and my family, I run shit. I'm the man and she do what I ask, not what the fuck I do!

⟡ Justin

Man, I know by the tone in Keenan's voice that something crazy has happened and ninety-nine percent of the time, it's because MyeZelle has his ass shook. She's the only one that can send my man into a frenzied state. Though, Lindsey has gotten him hot under the collar lately as well. My brother is wearing too many hats in the love department. I still haven't found out the results of him and Lindsey's blow-out, so I guess we'll catch up on that too today.

I don't have that problem, at least not in the beginning of my marriage. My wife lived the Amish lifestyle with her parents in some rural town outside Philadelphia. Once she turned eighteen, Carrina left and came to Minneapolis to start a new life. She worked hard and put herself through veterinary school and eventually opened her own 24-hour vet hospital where I met her. One of my bull mastiff's, Pebbles was running around the dog park and injured a hind leg in a freak accident. Long story short, Pebbles needed surgery and after Carrina saved her leg and life I wanted to thank her by inviting her out to dinner and the rest is history. She was a very naturally beautiful but unassuming woman. After a few years, I finally proposed, and we had a very simple ceremony as was her wish. We invited Keenan, MyeZelle, Victoria and the kids and exchanged our vows at the courthouse. Afterward, we all went out to eat, everyone went home and that was that! Carrina wanted it that way so I didn't force the issue, hell it saved me a lot of money so why would I argue.

Fast forward a couple years and she literally flipped a fucking switch on me! She went from jeans and tee on the weekends to designer this and designer that overnight! Don't get me wrong I love the new Carrina! It's the fucking attitude that has turned me totally off! This woman thinks she's a fucking socialite now, an Ivanka Trump or someone uppity bitch like that!

Carrina no longer works full time at the vet hospital. She hired two vets and an office manager to run the business for her so she could focus on more important things, shopping! Now that she has all this fee time, Rina complains how she needs more from me. She needs more attention, more vacations, more time out with friends. At some point, MyeZelle and Victoria tried to bring my wife into their circle but that didn't last long at all! Carrina has gotten caught up in this "white privilege" shit which caused an immediate halt to that sisterhood. Now I know both MyeZelle and Victoria can be hell on wheels but when they embrace you, you're a sistah for life! That's how they roll, and I love them both for it. MyeZelle has clearly gotten fed up with her based on the last few Sunday dinners we've shared. MyeZelle is a fair but very real woman and once you fuck up with her, there is no coming back from that.

I've gotten to the point where I don't try to hide my infidelities. I'm hoping that will push her ass right out the door. Keenan, MyeZelle and Victoria are three of the most important people in my life. With Carrina changing her entire personality, I really give two fucks anymore! I was smart enough to hide most of my assets before ever popping the question just in case my wife ever changed up on me and now, I'm glad I did! I regret ever marrying her ass now!

I was in a relationship for three years with Kadence before I met Carrina, and everything was good until Kadence started whining about me putting a ring on it. My thought then was if I wanted to put a ring on her hand, I would have done so, right?! Instead, I gave her ninety days to find another place to live and paid the first six months of her rent. Once she was moved in and comfortable, I blocked her ass from my phone, my social media pages, everything!

The crazy bitch couldn't get to me, so she showed up at my office, trashed it and created a whole scene. After having her ass arrested for trespassing, vandalism and domestic violence, I made sure security knew going forward, she was persona non grata! MyeZelle was able to acquire a permanent restraining order for me and I haven't seen that crazy broad since!

Kee thought I was an asshole for the way I treated her. I looked at it as just the opposite. I gave the woman whatever she wanted. I sent her and her girls on vacation twice a year. I took her out of the country on five separate occasions, paid off her college tuition and she still wanted more! Had she waited until I was ready, she would have been the one. But, because she jumped the gun, I sent her packing! Looking back, I should have married her psycho ass! She only went crazy after I broke it off with her. I thought I knew exactly what I was getting with Carrina, but this bitch went from Ms. Jekyll to Mrs. Hyde with the bat of an eye and a marriage license!

I've re-claimed the single life again for the most part. While my wife and I still live together, she has to know that it's over. I haven't touched her in months. Kee and I invested in a condo we call the "Spot". Some nights, I take two or three females there and never bother going home. I tell them up front that I'm married, and my wife knows I fuck around so if you're looking to fall in love and think you're going to break up a happy home, you're wasting your time! Some hoes get off on being around men with power, money and the idea of being a side chick so they don't care, it's just about being around you and breathing the same air you breathe! They don't get anything out of it but a wet ass the next morning and a "thanks for a good time" speech and I'll call you and sometimes gifts and money the pussy and neck game good! That's how I roll, no drama, no ringing my phone, questioning me, none of that bullshit!

For a while, I had a crush on Victoria. It was inevitable! I mean, we have dinner almost every Sunday at Kee and Mye's crib and the four of us would go on vacation, at least once a year before I got married. Victoria's only downfall is, she's too much like MyeZelle. You can't impose your will on that type of woman. It's just the opposite, they tend to impose their will on you! But Vic, if I could ever get her, I would change my ways for real. Some people think if you're white, stick with that and the same if you're black, its bullshit! If I ever get a chance with Victoria, I'm taking her mocha chocolate ass down aisle and handing over all my checkbooks!

We damn near got it cracking one night after the four of us were hanging out on a Saturday night. I know she wanted to get her swirl on, and I wanted her just as bad. You never say to a woman of that caliber any derogatory shit about what you're going to do to her unless y'all already have that established. That alcohol said, "go for it" and she squashed that shit in an instant. I've never been turned down by a woman that way. After reading me my rights, she made me feel even smaller by telling me all the things she would have done to and for me had I played my cards right! I've been chasing that pussy since, but she ain't going!

I lay around for a couple hours until Kee calls and tells me to meet him at "The Spot". The advantage for Kee with our spot, no hotel receipts for nosy ass MyeZelle to find while balancing their books. We have Merry Maids come in once a week to keep things fresh and clean. Whenever we have intimate parties, we hire a chef and bartender for the night.

The "Spot" is a two-bedroom condo but its 2,500 square feet and very spacious. It's less than ten minutes from Kee's crib. Its super convenient for me when I've had one too many at Sunday dinner and can't drive back to Eden Prairie when Carrina chooses not to tag along.

Keenan's car is already in the garage as I pull in. I find my boy drinking on a Corona and smoking a Newport! "Damn, I thought you cut them cancer sticks loose brother?!" I'm agitated because that shit stinks. Cigarette smoke gets into your clothes, hair, fucks up your furniture and walls, and the shit is unhealthy! "What the hell going on with you that made you go buy some damn cigarettes," I demand.

After finishing his cancer stick, Keenan explains that MyeZelle was out all night, giving him an excuse, she drank too much with Victoria and had to spend the night at her place. "Kee, that sounds about right. I mean, you know when the two of them get together and have their "waiting to exhale" moments, they get fucked up. I can see that happening. Why don't you buy it?" He gives me several reasons that make absolutely no sense at all! "Man, that's your conscience fucking with you cause of all the bullshit you're doing! MyeZelle ain't messing around on you man, that woman loves you! Now, if you would have told me that she tried to kill yo ass and that's what got you shook, that would make sense," I laugh! He joins in on the laughter and finally calms down.

After getting the MyeZelle issue out of the way, he hits me with the Lindsey drama! "You still got the girl's phone Kee," I ask in disbelief. He just nods his head yes. This motherfucker is really losing it! "What makes you think you can take that woman's phone, man you tripping! The pussy can't be that damn good!" It's like I'm talking to a brick wall! He's attempting to justify his actions but I'm not buying in.

"Kee, look brother, fucking around with this hoe is one thing, getting in your feelings over a piece of pussy is on another level. Have you ever thought about what would happen if MyeZelle finds out? She's gonna put your ass through the ringer! Did you forget that your wife is a lawyer with big ass connections all over the twin cities?!"

Keenan isn't hearing a damn thing I'm saying. "Man, I got MyeZelle, she doesn't know shit about me and Lindsey," he responds. "Yeah, alright, well I guess you got it all figured out brother. You're putting a lot of faith and trust in two women, one who really shouldn't mean shit to you after what you found out, and the other, your wife, can take everything you've been building, including your kids, your crib, hell man, even your damn dogs, not to mention your good name in this city alone brother!" Kee stares off into space for a few moments before commenting he has a plan. "I'm gonna set that bitch, Lindsey up," he finally responds. "Look man, I know how your brain works and right now, I'm telling you to leave Lindsey's white trash ass right where she is! It's too much pussy in this city for you to be stuck on one white girl. Dude, you have in-house pussy and you wanna risk it all over some white trash, you tripping Kee, you tripping big time man!" I leave it alone at this point cause he ain't trying to hear nothing I have to say and I'm wasting my time!

We spend the rest of the afternoon drinking beer and watching basketball. I've said everything I can to this man and given him the best advice I could offer, what he does with it is on him! I got a couple bankrolls on two games today so that's where my focus is now.

✑ MyeZelle

I spent most of the day in bed on Sunday resting and trying to wrap my head around everything that took place last night. Keenan was pissed, understandably so but once he returned home, his anger had dissipated. He'd missed dinner with the kids and I but it didn't matter. Neither Victoria nor Justin showed up so that gave me even more time to myself which was a good thing. I knew Justin would be with Kee if they both missed Sunday dinner and the more time spent away to cool down, the better things would be when he finally came home. There wasn't much conversation once Keenan did finally arrive home and it was just as well. I continued watching Discovery ID, he fell asleep as quickly as his head touched the pillow.

I went through my normal routine Monday morning, getting prepared for the day. After getting the kids off to school, I make a quick call to Vic to let her know I was on my way downtown. "Hey good morning," sounding chipper. "Well, someone sounds like they had a good night," Victoria responds. "Everything worked itself out. He and Justin hung out all day getting tipsy and watching the games. Girl, by the time Kee got home, he was too in it to be mad. He didn't talk much, hell I think our conversation lasted about ten minutes before he started snoring, so I was good. And this morning, he acted as if he'd forgotten the entire thing, at least I hope he has," I chuckle. Vic agrees that Keenan has probably forgotten about Saturday as well. I give Victoria a heads-up that I must meet with Ronald today to try and convince him that I cannot continue to represent him. "MyeZelle, I don't know what it's going to take for you to get through to him and now that you've given up the cookie, who knows what's next. You have to stop messing with this guy, the longer you allow this man to be a part of your life, the deeper he's going to insert himself. Mye, this shit is going to get very messy if you don't stop it now," she pleads. "I know Vic. There's just something about Ron that pulls me in, and I get I'm creating a monster, I just don't know how to stop it, shit I don't know if I want to. He gave me something that Keenan hasn't tried or just won't in years! The man is hung like Safaree, and I don't know what Safaree can do with his, but Ronald Henderson baby can get it errrdayyyy,"

I joke! Victoria lets out a long sigh. "I'm going to end it, I promise. I'll see you in the office later girl, love you Vic." With that I end the call and prepare myself to meet up with Ron.

Before calling Vic, I called Ron and asked that we meet downtown, he quickly and enthusiastically agreed. As I enter the Birchwood Café, I immediately spot Ron sitting at a table in the back talking on his phone. He stands as I approach and reaches out to hug me. His scent takes my breath away. "Good morning sweetheart," he whispers and kisses me softly on the cheek. After we sit, exchange pleasantries and place our orders, I dive right into the issue at hand. "Ronald, I have to be honest with you," I sigh. "What's happened with us just can't, it has to stop. You know my situation and you're my client. I could be disbarred. Will you please allow Victoria to take over your case or allow me to refer you to a very formidable colleague I've worked with in the past," I beg. Ron reaches across the table to hold my hand and gaze longingly into my eyes. "MyeZelle, if, and that's a big if; I allow your partner to take over my case, I want to be able to spend time with you." He is clearly missing the whole point! "Ron, what's the point of me recusing myself if I'm going to continue to see you," I ask pointedly! I continue, "I want to recuse myself so that I don't have to see you, I can't do this thing with you, Saturday was a mistake that I can't allow to happen again, do you not get that?!"

This man isn't even pretending to listen to me. "I want to be able to see you as much as possible. The only way I will allow Victoria or anyone else to take over my case is if you say you'll be with me, outside of your office. I mean, you can take off whenever you feel like it. You work for yourself. I know you're married with a family but if the nigga was treating you right, you would have never fucked with me from day one and you know it." He's one hundred percent right about the state of my marriage but that's neither here nor there. "Ron, that's blackmail! You can't force me to be with you," I counter with a raised voice. He refuses to take no for an answer. "Alright MyeZelle, tell me this, if I walk away right now, would that make you happy? I won't call or text, hell I'll hire a new law firm. That way you don't have to deal with me at all. Victoria doesn't have to take my case and I don't need you to recommend anybody. Is that what you want MyeZelle, the truth," he demands. I want to and should lie but I can't. In all honesty, if it weren't for my children, Keenan and I would already be divorced due to his numerous affairs. "No Ron, I can't say that I would be happy if you were to walk out of my life. I just don't know how this is ever going to work, its wrong but you're absolutely right, I want you as much as you want me, if not more. The fact that you know it, leads me to think that you would take advantage of the situation and use it against me the minute you don't get your way." He stops me from continuing. "What type of motherfucker do you think I am MyeZelle?! Don't let my past confuse you of the type of man I am today baby. The only people that I use my power and muscle on are niggas in these streets. I don't prey on women and damn sure don't abuse or misuse them. I'm still taking care of my aunt who struggled with that crack shit. You think that's the kind of man that preys on women?" Before I have time to answer, Ronald continues, "I'm a simple man to figure out. One side, I'm still that nigga who handle my business by any means necessary. That other side, I'm a family man and I take care of who and what I love. That much you should already know about me," concluding his impassioned speech.

We manage to get through breakfast and end our conversation on a lighter note. After walking me to my car, he tries reassuring me once again that he will never hurt me and just wants any time he can get. "So, what do want me to do MyeZelle? Would it be easier if I fire you as my lawyer and hire a new firm?" I explain to him that removing my firm would require an explanation to the judge as to why I need to recuse myself. "We should just keep things as they are, but I have to be more careful. "What's happening between us has the potential to become dangerous, not only for my personal wellbeing but my career. Do you understand?" "I understand baby and I'll always protect you and never jeopardize your career, okay? Now that we got that out of the way, when can I see you sweetheart," he asks with a smile. "I have to take care of some things back at the office but later this afternoon, we can get together after if you're not busy," I respond. "MyeZelle, sweetheart, whatever I'm doing, I can drop. I'm a boss too remember, I got people to handle shit!" I smile and he pulls me in for a very, long and passionate kiss. I literally want this man to fuck my brains out right now, but I have business to take care of. After parting ways, I rush to the office to give Vic the good news, part of it anyway.

"Hey Aliya," I address my assistant with a smile. "Good afternoon Mrs. Washington how was court", she enquires. "The usual pre-trial bullshit," we laugh in unison. I popped into Vic's office with a huge smile on my face, trying to mask my nervousness. "Hey girl, what's going on," I ask. "The question is, what's going on with you?" She continues, "you never called me this morning to let me know what happened at breakfast, but I see you're still alive, so what the hell happened?" "Mr. Henderson has agreed to follow by the rules I've set forth so I'm still representing him. He understands my position and has given up all hope that there could ever be anything between us," I lie. Vic is staring me down and I know why. "MyeZelle please! You think I really believe that! You and I both know damn well a man like that isn't just gonna give up and walk away, especially when he knows that your pussy gets hot at the mere sight of him, girl please!" I put on my best poker face trying to get Victoria to believe me, but she isn't buying what I'm trying to sell at all! "Well, believe what you want but Ron and I are good." I walk away before she can get another word in.

After getting some work done, I give Ron a call as promised. "What's up sweetheart," he says enthusiastically. "Hey, what's going on with you," I respond. We literally listen to each other breathe before he finally speaks up. "Are you still coming to see me sweetheart like you promised," he questions. "Yes, I'm leaving the office now. Where should I meet you?" "Its gonna be the same place baby. I'm working on something really special for us I think you you're gonna love it but I don't want to say anymore right now. Hit me when you pull up baby," and with that he hangs up.

"Alright ladies, I'm out of here," directing a quick goodbye to Aliya and Victoria. Aliya responds appropriately with a goodnight but does Vic, hell no! She prances towards me, "so where are you off to so early Mrs. THOT, I mean Mrs. Washington," laughing the entire time. I don't find it amusing at all! "I'm going to mind my business and I suggest you do the same Ms. Asshole," I quip in response. I add a "roll of the eyes" to further let her know that her comment was unwarranted and walk my happy ass out the door!

I'm not sure why I'm feeling nervous about meeting Ron this time. I've already spent the night with him but going to him straight after work almost makes me feel like I'm going to meet my man and I'm not comfortable with that feeling at all. I send Ron a quick text and as I walk toward the entrance of the club, he rushes out to greet me. I receive what has now become his signature greeting, a warm hug and kiss on the cheek and neck. "Come with me lady love." I just smile and follow. The club doesn't open until four, so it seems we're all alone and that causes my nerves to go into overdrive.

As we enter his upstairs suite, the smells immediately catch my attention, aroma of warm sugar cookies fill the air. Ron has an indoor picnic set up for us. He literally brought in some 3-inch indoor/outdoor green carpet that looks and feels like soft grass to lay over the carpet. There's a picnic basket with wine, cheese, fruit and various deli meats. I gotta say, this man really knows how to get to a woman's heart, his thoughtfulness and detail into the smallest of gesture to make this moment perfect is truly amazing!

"This is really beautiful Ron. You didn't have to go through all this trouble." "Doing something special for you isn't trouble. I've been crazy about you since the first day I walked in your office and asked you to save my ass from doing time," he chuckles.

We spend the next few hours chatting about life and where we want to be in the next year personally while snacking on cheese and sipping wine. We catch up on the last couple episodes of "Queen Sugar" on OWN that I've missed while cuddling. I literally could have spent another night in this man's arms, but I knew I couldn't. "I'm gonna have to take off Ron. I can't give off any vibes to my husband that something's going on." He relents and walks me out to my car. We kiss passionately and before saying goodbye, Ron whispers in my ear, "I'm gonna make you fall in love with me." He then backs up and just smiles. I smile back, jump in my car and drive away without looking back.

I once again hit up my favorite boutique to get a couple more items. This time, I plan on doing a little shopping for Mr. Henderson. That first night with Ron was amazing but I would have prepared myself better had I known I would end up in his bed. While the night was beautiful, I would have worn something sexier.

"Hey, where is my girl?" The owner always has unique pieces from up-and-coming designers along with well-known designers. "So where is Jackie?" "Mrs. Myzelle, we have everything ready. Jackie had to run out but she made sure you would have everything you need for your special night. Please check them out and let me know if there is anything else that we can do for you." "All seems in order Angela, thank you all so much!" And with that I'm off and running.

✑ Anniversary Weekend

Its 2:30 and the festivities start at exactly 7PM. Kee is home so hopefully he can help with putting the final touches together. "Hey Rosie," I smile a bit anxious because things don't seem to be in the order that I was hoping for this late in the day. "Are we running behind schedule, what's going on", I ask. "No, Mrs. M, all is well. We will have everything completed by 5:00. It's okay for you to head upstairs, it is all under control." "Thanks Rosie, glad I could count on you, see you in a short while." As I'm walking upstairs, I can hear Keenan whispering into his phone. I can't make out everything he's saying but I did get, "make sure whoever you get is discreet, she's a fucking lawyer so she's already paranoid brother. I don't want her to find out she's being followed." Who in the hell is he talking to why is he asking someone to follow me! Keenan must believe that I am having an affair, why else would he have someone follow me? I can't think about this right now. We have too much going on this evening. "Hey honey, is that your girlfriend on the phone," I laugh as I brush by him. I need to make some phone calls and take a hot soaking bath to get my mind right. After some much needed unwinding in the bath, I can now focus on getting myself together and finish up any last-minute details.

"Hey Vic, please tell me that you're on the way. I'm getting dressed right now." "I'll be there in about a half hour, and we need to talk about this Ron situation you have!" Victoria bringing Ron up right now is not a good sign. I love her but Vic can sometimes get loose with her tongue after a few shots of Patron. She obviously knows that I didn't break things off with Ron but Vic is my best friend so she should be on my side, right or wrong!

It's now one hour until all the festivities begin and I'm nervous but excited to see all of our closest friends and family come out to celebrate with us. Rosie has done a great job on the decorations. It looks like we really are back in the 70's. Crush red velvet bean bags surrounding the pool. Disco balls and strobe lights hanging from the trees and the DJ is playing all 70's music and disco tunes. This may surprise you but I'm a huge Bee Gees fan. I also love blues and old school R & B. I tolerate some hiphop. I've always been a huge fan of Tupac, NWA, Ice Cube and Snoop.

The area where the food is set up looks amazing! Rosie and her crew did a fantastic job. We have a seafood tower, fruit and veggie tower. Filet minion, beef ribs, pork ribs, boneless ribs. We even brought in some southern comfort foods. You know, greens and smoked turkey legs, dressing, baked macaroni, baked beans, mashed potatoes, black eyed peas. And we can't forget the desserts, everything, you can think of. Peach cobbler, black berry cobbler, lemon meringue pie, egg pie, red velvet cake, caramel and german chocolate cake! The bar is filled with the best vodkas, cognacs and tequilas. From Ciroc, Patron, Hennessey, all types of margaritas, imported and domestic beers, Ace of Spades Champaign, we got it all baby! Its going to be a night to remember or maybe not remember depending on your liquor consumption.

Its 7pm and most of our guests have already arrived and I'm the Queen of playing hostess. Vic is in the middle of the growing crowd laughing and smiling with Justin. "Hey sis, I need to steal you away from white knight for a minute," I joke. Before I could get into what I needed to talk to Victoria about, she interrupts me. "Not trying to spoil your night but don't be surprised if your boy toy pops his ass up!" "What do you mean if he pops his ass up, he doesn't know where I live, does he?" As she begins to answer, right on cue, here's Kee. "What are my two favorite ladies talking about?" "Just wondering where my husband has been hiding for the past hour." "Girl you know, even a party is networking for me. Anytime I can get a potential client, that's money for us. A happy wife is happy a life and your ass ain't cheap," Keenan laughs as he places his hand on the small of my back. I offer up a warm smile in return. I'm not sure if it's the drinks I've consumed or if I'm actually into my husband tonight.

It's close to midnight and the party doesn't appear to be ending anytime soon. Our parties usually last until the wee hours of the morning but I'm hoping by 2am everyone will have had their fill and go home. All our guests are having a great time, dancing, eating, most are mingling with a drink in hand, some couples are cuddling on chaise lounges and bean bags.

"What's up baby girl, you look super sexy tonight." It's Ron, what the hell is he doing here and how does he know where the fuck I live! This has to be some sort of bad dream! I mean I know I'm tired and a bit tipsy, but damn, am I hallucinating?! I turn around, "what are you doing here Ron! This is my home I share with my husband and our kids! You're fucking out of line, and I need you to

66

go now before... "What's up Mye, who's your friend?" Oh my GOD, this cannot be happening! I have to put on a poker face! "Honey, this is Ronald, one of my clients. I've spoken about Ron before. Don't you remember honey? Anyway, I invited him along with a few other clients that might pique your interest and I thought it would be great for him to come and maybe meet one of our single girlfriends, you don't mind do you honey?" "No baby, not at all. It's good to meet you man, my wife has told me some great things about how far you've come. You should be proud of yourself man." I quickly excuse myself because I feel as though I'm going to faint at this point. As I make my way over to Vic, I notice that those two are still talking but it looks like a very lighthearted conversation, thank GOD!

"Vic, why is Ron here? "How did you know he was coming? Did you do this Victoria and don't you fucking lie to me," I demand! "MyeZelle, have you lost it?! Hell no, I would never do anything like that! Think about it Mye, he followed you to my house, but you have no idea when he started following you. He has obviously followed you home at some point! Don't get all nervous and Keenan pick up on the shit. Let's go get a drink and mingle. You have to act like nothing's wrong Mye," Victoria advises. I explain to Vic how I overheard Keenan on the phone asking someone to follow me. "Look Mye, Kee doesn't know shit right now, he's just snooping around because you stayed out all night and the asshole knows what he's doing so he has a guilty conscience. You gotta keep it together right now. I'm by your side, just act normal!"

This bullshit is totally freaking me out, but Victoria is right! I can't give Keenan any indication that something is wrong! Vic and I grab another drink and make our way back over to Kee and Ron.

I can't shake the nervousness in my stomach walking over so I pace myself. My heart is racing, I'm tipsy and I can't be sure but I'm almost positive that my blood pressure is through the roof right now! "Hey honey, what are you to guys up to?" My mind is going a million miles a minute and I'm damn near going to bite my bottom lip off at this point. Who's going to speak first, and when they do, what in God's name are they going to say?

"Hey love, I was just talking to Ron about life. Baby, if a man like Ron can turn his life around the way he has, no man should have any excuse to not be successful. I mean, baby I need him to work for me," as he laughs boisterously. I can see Ron simmering! Keenan is a fucking asshole, and I don't have time for his narcissistic bullshit at the moment! Vic, always one with a comeback responds, "why would this man work for your snooty ass when he has people working for him Keenan. You should probably put down the Henny and pick up the Fiji water Boo!" The three of us laugh but Keenan shakes his head and replies tartly, "it was a joke Victoria, it's a party, take off the lawyer hat for a minute." I have to interject before things go all the way left! "Kee, honey, I need to speak with you. Will you two excuse us for a moment." Keenan and I make our way through the patio doors and into my home office for a private conversation.

"Kee, just because you have a booming business doesn't mean you have to throw it in someone else's face. What makes you think that man isn't pulling down just as much money as you, if not more? Don't be such a prick, this isn't an architectural seminar, it's a party so act like it," I demand! I don't know what made me get so fucking bold to defend Ronald, but Keenan's ass deserved it! I just don't' get how a man thinks because he takes care of his wife and kids, it gives him the right to boast about it to anyone at any given time, its obnoxious! I understand that he makes more than a lot of people but this whole white, preppy, "I'm so much better than you attitude" has become redundant and I'm over it! Kee doesn't respond and walks out. I stand alone in my office for several minutes trying to take in everything that's going on. Once I've calmed down, I return to the party, not so much upset with Ronald and the surprise pop-up but more disgusted by husband's asinine attitude. After gathering my composure, I return to Ronald and Victoria to gauge Ron's demeanor.

"So Ron, why didn't you bring your significant other with you, she's more than welcome to join you. The party is just getting started." "Oh no Ms. Washington, I don't have anyone special in my life, maybe I can find her here. I kinda got a feeling I've already spotted her." I think I almost fainted. He's a very bold one, I give him that. I may need a blunt to handle the rest of this night! This baby is really trying to stake his claim. Hell, it wouldn't surprise me if they got into a pissing contest at this point! "Well, I do have a few single friends here who would consider you as a great catch, so get your drink on and enjoy the party!" I walk off before he has a chance to respond.

I finally get a chance to pick Victoria's brain again about how Ron knows where I live and how did he know we were having our anniversary party tonight. The response she gives still doesn't satisfy me in the least. I know when Vic is lying. What I don't understand is why. Am I too drunk and just being paranoid but I really feel like my best friend is totally lying to me! "Vic, don't bullshit me, why would you say that he may pop up and soon as I turn around, that's exactly what happens. How does he know where I live?" Victoria is laughing but refuses to answer the question. "You know what Vic; I hope you didn't give this man my home address out of some jealousy type shit cause this is not cool at all." Victoria's smile is now upside down. "Mye, I answered that question the first time you asked. You should know me a lot better than that! The man has connections in high and low places! He could have been following you or paid someone to do it. Hell, MyeZelle, he can go online, pay a fee for a background check and get your address! Get it together sis!"

I let it go and just immerse myself in tonight's festivities. I notice Ronald has started to mingle a bit. I catch him flirting with my little sister Tasha, who flew in from Chicago to hang for the weekend. He's definitely not her type but judging by their body language and laughter, he's entertaining her. I see my husband has found a couple white girls with plastic body parts to occupy his time and Justin is the life of the party as usual. I ask the DJ to put on some stepping music, R Kelly to begin with so we can dance off some of this alcohol. With all the drama and bullshit going on, losing myself in great music and dancing is just the thing that I need at this moment!

Keenan has been spending most of his time catering to every single woman that was invited. Justin and Victoria are getting their step on, and Ron seems to be really putting the moves on my sister. I would love to go over and cuss him out, but I have to keep my composure.

Keenan interrupts the music to propose a toast. "Hey everyone, I'd like to have your attention for a moment. I want to make a toast to my wife and let her know just how much I appreciate her. Sweetheart, I want to thank you for putting up with me all these years. You're a great wife, awesome mother and a kick-ass lawyer. Thank you for being and staying a part of my life." Everyone claps and cheers as he walks over and gives me a kiss.

Once the DJ turns the music back up, Keenan heads in one direction and I go the opposite direction. Victoria looks white girl wasted as what has become a normal routine for her. She's laid out on a chaise lounge, drink in one hand, a plate of food resting on her lap and screaming into her cellphone. I'm guessing it's her date that never showed. "Hey girl, what's up," I ask curiously. "Who were you just snapping on?" She looks at me angrily, "some bitch just called my phone questioning me about Gary. It was his ex-wife wanting to know if we were back together. Can you believe that shit Mye? First of all bitch, don't call a woman's phone asking about your ex! Two, he obviously told your pathetic ass that we are back together and three, I suggest you lose my number quickly!" I'm cracking up, "Vic, did you tell that lady all of that," I ask still snickering. "Hell yeah, I told her all of that and waited for a response for a couple of seconds and when she didn't reply, I hung up! Now Mye, you know I don't play any games when it come to my personal or professional life. If she didn't know, she does now. He obviously said something to her that made that witch get enough courage to call me. What I'm wondering is when was he going to tell me so we both can know!" Vic and I have a good laugh at both the ex and Gary's expense. We don't give it too much attention and return to the party. By 4am, everyone has gone home with the exception of Justin and Victoria. Justin crashes in the family room and Victoria finds the guestroom my sister was occupying to get some shut eye. Where Tasha went is anyone's guess but she's more than capable of taking care of herself. I send her a text, and with that out of the way, drag myself upstairs to bed.

Overall, the party was a great success. I actually picked up two clients that work for Keenan, so I was extremely happy. Rosie fixed a great brunch for us and by 1pm, everyone had their bearings.

❧ Back to Reality

I'm still feeling the effects of everything that went down Saturday, but its Monday and I have a ton of paperwork and phone calls to make once I hit the office. After arriving, I notice Vic is nowhere to be found which is unusual. She'll be my first call! As I enter my office, I see non other that Ron! What the hell! "What are you doing here," I demand! "MyeZelle, we need to talk, I'm in some trouble." As we move into my office I can feel my anxiety building, like I have a bullfrog stuck in my throat and a hundred butterflies going nuts in my stomach. I ask my assistant to hold all my calls and proceed to my office. He closes the door behind us and locks it. Just as I turn to ask him not to, he grabs me and pulls me tightly into his arms.

"Do you know why I came to your house on Saturday?" I shake my head no. "I wanted to see just how happy you really are. From what I could tell, you're not. That yellow nigga not doing it for you no more. He don't even seem into you. I saw him spending more time with the white women than he was with you. I can make you happy MyeZelle." "Ron, I really don't appreciate you showing up to my home and I don't appreciate you coming to my office without an appointment. I've told you more than once that I must be careful. You can't be doing this type of shit! And while we're on the subject of my anniversary party, what the fuck was going on with you and my baby sister!" Ron glares at me for a few moments. "What MyeZelle, do you think I would hit on your sister? I knew who she was after talking to her for a minute! Why do you think I spent all that time with her? I'm sure everyone, including your bum ass yellow husband thought we hit it off and that's just how I played it. I told her that I was in love with a woman but I don't know if we'll ever be together because of her obligations to her husband." "You spent hours with her Ronald, what else did you talk about because she told me everything," I lie! "What do you want to know Myezelle, yeah I told your sister that if I wasn't in love with someone else, she would be a woman I would be interested in." I immediately rebut, "Tasha told me everything you said, including how you would take her home and have her calling your fucking name for hours!" "Look sweetheart, yeah we flirted a little and I talked some shit but that was it. Hell, you were right there so don't act like you saw me doing something out of order and I didn't come here for that. I came to see if my pussy the same way it was last time I left it. You better not had fucked that yellow nigga I don't give a damn if he do got papers on you!"

Without giving me an opportunity to respond, Ron grabs my hair and forcefully kisses me. I try to resist for a brief moment but he's much too strong for me and I can feel his nature rising. My juices have already drenched my thong, and my pussy is throbbing painfully. He puts his hand between my legs and literally picks me up by the pussy and carries me over to my desk. This is so inappropriate on so many levels but damn I don't want him to stop. He bends me over my desk, rips my thong completely off and shoves his cock inside me. No foreplay, just fucking me as punishment for having an anniversary party. For an instant, I felt as though I was being assaulted. I don't know why that thought came to mind but there was no feeling of love or lust, just anger. I'm not stopping him; shit feels too damn good although he's beating my pussy like I've never felt before. After what seems like forever, he pulls out, flips me over and pin my legs high in the air. Ron sits in my chair and starts finger fucking me slowly, lovingly as if his anger has been washed away. He then slips his tongue inside and kisses and licks my clit until my legs are shaking uncontrollably. I haven't cum that hard or that many times in a while! He then slides his large cock back in but now he's not fucking me for punishment, he's slow rolling and whispering in my ear how much he loves me and how I need to be with him. Tears begin to roll down my face. I'm in a sea of emotions and I don't know what to do. Am I crying because his love making sends me somewhere? Is it because I now know that I have absolutely lost control of this situation? Is it that I've literally fallen in love with the gangster in him, the dick or both? I'm moaning and screaming "Oh Ron, ooohhh daddy" and he's grunting and growling, "shit this my pussy, this mine! You better not give that bitch nigga no more of my pussy!"

"Knock, knock, knock!" Oh GOD, I'm dead I think, panicking! He doesn't stop right away and now the knocks have turned into banging! "Ron baby please," I beg him. He finally concedes and allows me to get up. My desk is a complete disaster and my office smells like we've been on a fuck fest for hours. I rush to my private bathroom, get myself together as much and as quickly as possible. He follows me and does the same. The knocking has stopped but whoever is on the other side of that door hasn't left because my private line is now ringing off the hook! I beg Ron to stay in the bathroom but that was wasted breath. He calmly walks back into the office and sits as if he's just a regular client on a scheduled appointment.

After ten minutes or so, I've finally calmed down and gotten myself together enough to call my assistant to see what the hell is happening on the other side of the door. I may be tough at times but I'm definitely not stupid!

"Aliya, what's going on? I asked for all my calls to be held." "Yes, I know Mrs M, but Ms. Vic forced me to call repeatedly after you wouldn't answer the door, she seems furious. She's pacing in her office!" After I calm Aliya down, I buzz Vic. "What's going on boo," trying to be as cool as possible. "Open you're fucking door is what's going on!" She hangs up and I have no other choice but to face her, it's not like I can keep him hiding in my office for the next eight hours! First, I straighten my desk and before I can gather the papers that's been tossed this woman is knocking again. I also spray a touch of Febreeze and light a couple candles to mask the sex smell.

"Good morning Victoria," I say with a slight smile. She brushes right past me after slamming the door behind her. Is this bitch tweaking or what? "You know Mye, I don't know what the hell you and Ron right here don't get but you're married! You have kids and if the two of you don't cut this bullshit out right now, you're going to find yourself in a really fucked up situation!" I know she's right but before I can try to explain, Ron interjects. "Look Vic, this has nothing to do with you. MyeZelle is a grown ass woman, I'm a grown man and what we got going on is none of your fucking business! Check yourself! Worry about who you not fucking!" He walks over, kisses me on the neck and says he'll be back to pick me up for lunch. Ron then lets his driver knows he's ready and abruptly walks out like a King!

Vic and I have a heated argument that lasted over an hour. After all the yelling and screaming we decide to call a truce and get back to the business at hand, being lawyers! Its already 11:45 and I really haven't gotten anything done. At this point my mind is so overwhelmed I can't focus on shit anyway. It's time to call it a day!

I'm on my way to my car and Ron and his driver are parked next to my car and at this point I'm not at all surprised by his presence. "What are you doing here," I ask, perplexed. "I said, I would pick you up for lunch. Why are you leaving the office so early any fucking way? Are you gonna let that bullshit with Victoria rattle you? Look, you don't have to worry about Victoria, I know how to handle females like that." "I'm not going anywhere with you Ron;

this is too much. It's already gotten too crazy and the last thing I need is my best friend and business partner flipping out. Please move out of my way," I ask. "So, now what MyeZelle, Victoria runs you when dude not around, huh? Why you keep playing with me Mye, I'm not your fucking husband and I told you, I know how to handle Vic! Get in the car now MyeZelle and stop looking at me like you're scared. I would never hurt you, I told you that, now let's go! I got something I need you to see!" I'm not sure if it's the multiple orgasms, the fight with Victoria or the way Ron just spoke to me, but I give in. I have zero fight left in me today and the crazy thing is, I feel safer with him than with my husband and Vic's crazy ass right now so why not!

Once we get into his car, Ron makes it very clear exactly how he's feeling. "I told you I was coming back for lunch, and you want to duck out on me? I don't know what type of guy you think I am, but I'm a man of my word and if you say you're going to give me some time, I expect you to do the same and keep your word MyeZelle."

Ron has basically forced me into his car and while I'm feeling a bit uneasy, I don't have a genuine fear for my safety with him. It's the total opposite, I actually feel very secure and protected when I'm with this man. This thug, rough-neck side of Ron turns me on and although I know its wrong it feels so damn right! That gangsta shit is something I've never been able or wanted to escape from, its embedded somewhere deep within my soul. "Ron, I get it okay, now will you please tell me where we are going and why were you just waiting in the parking garage for me, you're starting to freak me out!" He gives me a smile but says absolutely nothing. Vic told my ass to leave this man alone but no, I wanted some fucking excitement, the attention I haven't been receiving at home! We don't drive for very long and we're at one of the most expensive buildings downtown. I keep my composure as best I can at this point but once the car stops, I'm overcome with fear! This isn't a club setting, it's a private residential building.

"Let's go baby." Does Ronald really think I'm okay with just going anywhere with him! "I don't know where I am and I'm starting to have a bad feeling about you and this entire situation, I'm afraid! Where are you taking me," I demand, screaming at this point! Ronald looks at me, smirks and says, "I'm not trying to hear that shit! Get out the car Mye and let's go girl, stop being so scary Chi-town!" My heart has officially sunk into my stomach. This is what I deserve for allowing my needs to come before my vows. He holds me very close as we enter the building. All I can think, Ron's walking me to my death. That may seem a bit dramatic but he's a very intimidating man even with a smile on his face and I've already gotten a preview of his anger.

Once we're on the elevator I began to beg and plead for my life. I can't leave my babies, God Almighty, please help me! I'm praying like I've never prayed before, hopefully GOD is listening! The elevator chimes, "8th floor". He escorts me off and whispers in my ear, "babygirl, I could never ever hurt you, I love you too fucking much, now let's go. I have a surprise for you." Well, that's a load off my mind, not!

Ron opens the door to this spacious, open floor plan penthouse. It's beautiful on first glance! There's no way in hell he would harm or kill me here, would he? "Come on Mye, relax baby. The only way I could get you here was to kidnap your beautiful ass," he laughs. I finally settle my nerves briefly to ask what we are doing here and more importantly, why the hell was it so important for him to bring me here! After escorting me over to this beautiful living area with a two-story fireplace, we finally sit. I can't comprehend what's going on right now or what this man's plan is but I also cannot get over this amazingly beautiful apartment! A woman definitely lives here and that thought immediately angers me! Did he just bring me to some woman's home to make a fucking point?

"Why am I here Ron and whose home is this? I want to go and I want to go, now! Take me to my car right now!" I stand up as if barking orders at him will deter Ron from whatever it is he has planned. He laughs again and tells me to calm the fuck down because again, "you ain't taking yo fine ass nowhere until I say so! Now if you're done with all the drama shit, how do you like it," he asks. "How do I like what, being fucking kidnapped, threatened, and having my pussy beat to chopped meat? I don't like any of it Ronald!" "Babygirl, this is our house, mine, yours, the kids, your kids. My brother and sister pop in from time to time when there at one of the clubs and don't need to drive. We have dinner here once a week, mostly on Sundays. This our spot downtown to chill when we want to just hang out on the weekends together like a family, you know what I mean? My private rooms at the clubs are not suited for family gatherings, you know what I'm saying." I'm pretty sure my mouth is wide open, and I'm hoping I'm not drooling from shock at this point. What the fuck is he talking about? Family, my kids, his siblings; say what now?! I feel like I'm in the twilight zone! "What are you saying Ron? None of this is making sense. I have a family, a home and kids already established and what am I supposed to do with everything you're telling me right now?" Ron takes my hand we walk down this beautiful hallway lined with photos of his family. There are photos of him along with his sister, brother and late parents. There are photos of, I'm assuming his aunt and him through the years. It's crystal clear by the way Ron speaks of his family and the photos, he is all about family and loves them deeply. I spend a few minutes just browsing through each photo before following Ron into this beautiful master suite. It's decorated in aqua, cream and peach colors. Everything is soft and feminine.

It has an aquarium that surrounds this beautiful king sleigh bed. There is at least one hundred fish or more swimming on either side and on top. I can imagine myself waking up to something like this each morning, I'm speechless. He opens the floor to ceiling patio doors to reveal a spacious outdoor lounging area, complete with an outdoor kitchen and bar, the entire length of the penthouse. Most of the patio is covered in lush trees for privacy.

The master bath is just as beautiful. It has the same color scheme as the bedroom. His and her vanities along with a separate water closet, rainfall shower and jacuzzi garden tub. I'm in awe, I can't front, the man has excellent taste. He wastes no time, grabs my hand and ushers me back down the hallway and upstairs to three additional bedrooms, each with their own private full baths. One bedroom is decorated in soft pink and fuchsia colors. There are two queen sized round rotating beds on each end of the room both complete with a vanity a mirror. There's a large double desk with chairs facing floor-to-ceiling windows. The second bedroom has a rugged outdoorsy décor. The furniture is cherry wood. A king-sized bed sits center with wildlife print and a small living area with a pair of plush rockers with leopard print throws on each and facing a massive 85" flat screen. I'm assuming this bedroom is for aunt or guests, considering the rockers. The third bedroom is a boy's dream. Two sets of full-sized bunk beds decorated in blue bandana comforters. There's a large black entertainment center with a pair of gaming chairs and consoles along with a flat screen larger than the one in the "wildlife" room. Ron is the sort of man you would think of when you think of someone of buying a penthouse of this magnitude. The décor alone is out of a fairytale. The master suite is any couples' dream, calming, relaxing and very soothing. The kids' rooms are a dream. My children have great bedrooms but, my boys would never leave a room with a flat screen that size and gaming consoles! My girls would have more arts and crafts than they could handle! Even Vic would love that "wildlife" room! After the tour, we return downstairs to the living area for a drink.

After a long and intense conversation and back and forth about why he's holding me here, Ron finally gets to the point of all this. "Babygirl, I need you in my life and not just when I can get a damn appointment. I don't want or need you to be my lawyer anymore. I want you to be my girl, my woman, my rider, my wife." I don't know what I can possibly say to this man part do you not understand, I have a family. I can't just throw everything I've worked all my life for because you want what you want. Not only that but most men want what they cannot have. Even if I did leave my husband to be with you, there's no guarantee you would still want me! It's only fun when you have to chase it Ron and I will be left alone to pick up the pieces of a life I've worked so hard to build." "I know it's crazy and it's a lot to take in. I want you and not because I don't have you, I want yo ass cause I love you MyeZelle. Look, I'm not asking you to move in today but let me show you one more thing", checking his watch. Ronald hasn't heard anything I've said and my will to protest has all but disappeared.

As we head back to the patio off the master suite, Ron hands me a large manilla envelope. "Don't open it yet, let me fix a little something first." It's a warm beautiful afternoon and the fresh air is much needed. As Ron whips together drinks, I ask Alexa to play Bobby Womack. "Alright baby, now you can open the envelope and you will see just how serious I am", he bolsters. My hands are shaking so Ron does the honors. "It's a Deed, this place is yours alone. One more thing, there's a safety deposit box in your name with six million dollars in it. I'm gonna add to it but that's a start. I had my accountant set it up, but you will need to go to the bank to give him the rest of your info, so everything is legit." I'm sure the tears flowing down my face wasn't quite the reaction Ronald was expecting but that's all I could muster. "I don't know what to say, it's too much, I can't." Ron doesn't seem to care that I don't want any of the gifts he's bestowed upon me. "You do something to me MyeZelle. I've never wanted a woman the way I want you. I can have damn near any woman I want but the only one I want is you. I don't how long it takes, when you're ready, I'll be right here, now stop crying and have a drink sweetheart."

I love a stiff tequila sunrise and Ron makes it just right. We just sip and stare at one another for what seems like forever but only a few minutes pass. "Will you make me another drink please", I smile shyly. He lifts me off the lounge chair and guides me over to the bar. "I want you to make our drinks. You need to get used to everything here, including how to make my shit right," he laughs. I mean really, what's so hard about two cubes of ice and a double shot of Hennessey. I'm finally relaxing after a couple drinks and we're talking, laughing and enjoying one another's company as any normal, happy couple would. Time has started to slip away and after the fourth drink, I'm totally impaired and he knows it.

We walk back into the bedroom, and he points to one of the walk-in closets. "Open it and take a look inside." I stumble a bit but make my way. As I open the doors and step inside, I see lingerie to one side, women's clothing on the other side. Towards the back, there are women's shoes. At least twenty pairs of pumps, ten pairs of boots. Everything is coordinated by colors. As I turn around, Ronald is there standing with a broad smile on his face. "This is all yours babygirl." I don't know what to say at this moment. This man has my head spinning and it's definitely not the tequila! He reaches for a red nightie, "put this on for me. I just want to make sure I got your size perfect." I try to object but to no avail.

I walk as straight as possible into the bathroom. I sit at the vanity and look in the mirror. I look drained, drunk and totally out of it. I grab some towels and jump in the shower. Wow, he has sponges, loofas and even my damn Caress bodywash ready. I'll give him this, the man hasn't missed a beat when it comes to what a woman needs. I spend about a half hour under the rain shower, just trying to get my bearings back. It was worth it as I feel like a new woman, still a little tipsy but refreshed none the less. I lotion and slide into this beautiful silk nightie. As I get set to return to the bedroom, I notice Ron has slipped some red fur hills just inside the doorway. I slide them on and of course, perfect. Alright, I'm as ready as I ever will be!

Ron wastes no time as I enter the bedroom. He's totally naked and his dick is standing at attention. My God, this man has a body that can make a woman cum on site. He pulls me onto the bed, and we start kissing passionately. As he spreads my legs apart, my pussy starts throbbing as if I didn't get enough this morning. I moan and purr like I haven't been touched in months. His hands are so warm and gentle as he slowly rugs my clit. Sliding two fingers in and out of me, I start to moan louder. He slowly goes down and his tongue darts in and out of me, I let out sounds I didn't know I had inside me. He doesn't stop until I cum. He slowly crawls back up kissing and sucking on my nipples and thrusts his huge cock inside and I began to shake once more. After some time, he gets up, turns me over and puts me on my knees, "don't move and don't look back." The tone of his voice is commanding, and I oblige. I feel his fingers once again inside me and my entire body is shaking in ecstasy. He takes his fingers out, spread my lips open and inserts a dildo then turns it on. I'm feeling so weak, yet this feels so fucking good. I throw my ass back on the dildo while he thrusts it in and out. Before I know it, he's trying to put his huge cock in my ass! I beg for him not to, but he just keeps pushing slowly until he's finally all in. "Babygirl, throw that fat ass back on yo dick! Tell me how much you love yo dick Mye. I need to know baby, shit! You love me Mye, tell me baby!" He's grunting and I'm moaning, screaming in pleasure, it's so fucking good I'm literally crying tears. "Yes Ron, I love you baby, honey I love you", I scream! He pulls my hair, "yeah baby call me daddy, you mine, you hear me, mine! You my dirty lil slut baby, tell me!" Okay, I'm a little taken aback by the demand to be called daddy and being called a slut, but we are fucking after all! "I love you daddy, I'll be your dirty little slut daddy, I'll be anything you want daddy I promise!" And with that, one last giant thrust from him and scream from me and it's over! We both collapse on the bed for a short time.

"Babygirl, can you please fix us some drinks?" I nod and do as he instructs. I'm not sure if Ron is back or if Lucifer's still here but I don't want to piss either one of them off, so I comply. I quickly clean myself up and get our drinks. After handing Ron his drink and downing mine, I get us another refill. When I return, I see a look of concern on his face as he gestures me to sit beside him. "Mye, listen to me baby, I would never hurt you or do anything I know you wouldn't want. And all the nasty shit I said, that's just love making baby. I would never disrespect you in that way outside of our bed, only when I'm banging my pretty pussy or that fat ass," he chuckles. Well, that's a relief! As our conversation delves deeper into our wants and needs, it's the perfect time to let Ronald know what I absolutely am unwilling to do!

"Just please tell me that you're not into that BDSM shit, cause I'm not and I'm also not into threesomes!" Ronald stares in disbelief. "Mye, you trying to tell me you never had a threesome?" I pause but I don't lie, "yes, several, a long time ago, before my children were born, while I was in college. It's not something that I'm into anymore and if that's something you need, I'm the wrong person you Ron. Never ask me, do you understand?" "Sweetheart, I would never ask nor demand anything of you that you don't want. You all the woman I need. Shit, you more than enough freak for me. I didn't think you would let me hit that back, I just wanted to test how far I could go."

By the time Ron drops me back at my office, its after 7:30 and I'm sore, tired and completely drained. I don't know if I can even drive home at this point, I'm so weak! After sitting in my car and just going over today's events, I finally muster the strength to get my drive home.

✑ Keenan

So, my wife is just now bringing her ass home, not answering calls all day. This is the very reason I need Justin to find out what's going on. I'm in the garage waiting on her to pull up. "Hey Ms. MyeZelle, how the fuck was your day?!" I pulled her car door damn near off. I don't know why she's so shocked. I've called her office and cell both at least twenty times. "So, what's up baby, I thought your ass was dead, I've been calling you all damn day long. The kids' homework is finished. We've had dinner and all that, so where the fuck have you been?" I don't give her a chance to lie to me this time. "We're going upstairs to talk, don't worry about the kids, they're already settled in the for the night!" I grab her by her left arm and drag her ass upstairs to our room. She's questioning me about our kids, can she go talk to them before we go in our room. No bitch, you get none of that, it's time to answer some questions!

Once where in our room, I lock the door behind us. "So, you wanna tell me where the fuck you been cause after calling yo ass so many damn times, I started calling Vic. She didn't know where the fuck you were and don't even try to run that bullshit to me that you were with her cause it's a lie. I don't believe you were with her the last time you pulled this damn stunt. And don't give me that excuse that you've been at the office cause I actually went to the office and the only one there was Aliya!" MyeZelle remains stunned by my anger but silent.

I don't give MyeZelle a chance to respond before I start ripping her fucking clothes off. I know something's going on, it's all over her face! I wanna back hand her so fucking bad but she's too light skinned and I'm not trying to go jail! MyeZelle is now balling, and I feel no sympathy. My yelling has alarmed the kids and they're now banging on our door, terrified! "Go get your shit together while I take care of my kids." After MyeZelle locks herself in the bathroom, I open the door for my boys. "Hey guys, sorry for yelling, your mom and I just had a little disagreement. She's fine, just working too hard, and we need her home with us, right?" The twins nod in unison and I usher them back to bed. I can't go back in there with MyeZelle, I'm too angry and we've never had an argument that rattled my children. I do myself a favor and leave!

My head is banging from anger so I guess I will take it out on the white girl. I pull up to Lindsey's place where I can get some quick attention. I do have to return that bitch's cellphone anyway. I'm ready to turn my key but she immediately opens the door. "What's up my little blonde bombshell", I laugh!

She just glared and said, "good evening Kee, come on in, I was just running to the store but it can wait now that you're here." I grab a seat on the sofa and start scrolling through her phone to get her nervous. My wife has pissed me off, so I'll take my frustrations out on this lying bitch. I send Aryah a text asking her to call me, I sit and wait. In less than a minute, my phone starts ringing. "Hey, what's up Aryah", speaking loudly enough for Lindsey to hear the conversation. She looks pissed and that's just how I want her ass. I can't believe this hoe thought she could play me, me?! "Aye, I want you to stop by Lindsey's right now seeing as though you're not busy. I thought we could all have a drink and you girls could have a meaningful conversation and work things out like the ladies that you are." I can feel the hesitancy on Aryah's part, but this isn't about them, this shit is about me right now! I don't give a damn about either of these bitches' emotions. "Mando, I don't think that's a very good idea. Lindsey and I are not on speaking terms and I'm not comfortable being around, I'd like to fucking strangle her if anything!" Nothing she says means anything to me. "So, are you saying fuck me Aryah, is that what you're saying? I thought you wanted to see me?" Now I know I got her ass; a good guilt trip works every time on these ditzy ass broads. "I'm not sure why Lindsey has to be a part of this but sure Mando, will you give me an hour?" I agree and walk over to the bar where Lindsey is downing shots of Absolute back-to-back.

"What's wrong little Lindsey, you don't want to share your Mando with that fine ass Aryah?" I glare at her waiting for a response, but she remains silent. "I mean, you've been sharing the pussy so the only way to make it right, I want to fuck your best friend. Though, I'm not sure she wants to be your best friend now, you know with you fucking her husband in they crib and all!" After downing two more shots of Absolute, Lindsey drops to her knees.

She knows what the fuck I like, when and how I like it! See, if my wife did this shit, we wouldn't have a damn problem! I sit on a bar stool, unzip my pants and pull out my dick. Lindsey doesn't hesitate, she immediately deep throats! Her head game is A1. I should put this bitch on Porn Hub! She sucks and licks for a while before stopping suddenly. "I'll be right baby." Lindsey disappears into the bedroom for a couple of minutes and comes back with her tongue sticking out. "What the hell is that glowing in your mouth", I demand. She doesn't respond, just drops back to her knees and picks right back up where she stopped. "Shit baby, that damn thing is vibrating," I yell. That shit felt so good I had to stand with my back against the wall for balance. Grabbing the back of head with both hands, I face fuck her about five minutes before making her stop. "Suck on my nuts, slowly, not hard. Yeah, just like that. Yeah, that shit feel good. Put that dick back in yo mouth and swallow." I face fuck her a few more minutes before pulling out and skeeting that shit all over face. "Go grab me a towel and clean yourself up before Aryah gets here." Lindsey does as she's told and after she cleans me, I relax on the sofa and turn on ESPN. "Fix me a drink and come over and sit by me so we can talk." After Lindsey returns with my drink, I run a script on her ass.

"So, Lindsey listen baby, you cheated on me and you know I don't play that shit right? And the fact that you did it with your girl's husband, in her bed is fucked up so I gotta punish you. If you do everything I ask, I might keep you around but if you don't, I'm through fucking with you and I'll make Aryah the new side piece, understand?" She's crying hysterically but I don't give a damn! Lindsey has to know her place and I have to, as a man, remind her of that!

The doorbell rings and I decide to answer the door. "Yo, go get your face together and cut out all that damn crying, we about to have a good time tonight!" Upon opening the door, I can't help but admire her beauty. The broad is gorgeous! "What's up Aryah," I say, as I kiss her on the cheek. "Come on in lady." She smiles and walks in. "You looking like a treat Ms. Aryah, would you like a drink?" "Um, where is Lindsey, I thought she was here," she asks. "Yeah, she's here, she'll be out in a minute. Don't be nervous lady, I won't let little Lindsey hurt you. I brought y'all together so the two of you can kiss and make up, literally," I laugh. Lindsey finally brings her emotionally unstable ass back into the living room. I watch as they both glare at one another. Aryah is seething and Lindsey appears frightened. I finally cut the tension, "ladies, I didn't bring the two of you together for a wrestling match. You know how we men say, "bros before hoes", you ladies have to get on that same level. Never let a dick come between a true friendship!" Lindsey baby, grab the skittles dish, let's have some fun!"

The "skittles dish" is a mixture of pills; mollies, X, LSD, GHB, Fentanyl, Rohypnol, anything you can think of. Lindsey also enjoys a little powder up her nose along with a "Loud" blunt. I find a decent hip hop station to set the mood and usher both girls over to the bar. "Lindsey, you owe Aryah a sincere apology for fucking her husband, you owe me one too but I'll wait for mine," I chuckle. I almost feel sorry for Lindsey because she looks totally defeated. They both remain silent, standing on either side of me and my patience is starting to run out. "Look, if y'all don't want to enjoy a night with me, shit I can hit downtown to find two more that will. You know what, fuck it I'm out!" I finish my drink and proceed toward the door. "Mando wait," Aryah pleads, "you know I want to spend time with you. Just tell me what you want me to do, and I'll do it!" I wait for Lindsey to speak up. "Keenan, you know I don't want you leave but can you please just tell me why she's here," Lindsey pleads. "I'm here for Mando because he called me and asked me to come. I'm surprised you're not at my home right now with my husband or have you moved on to someone else's husband cunt," Aryah screams! "Aryah calm down," I yell! "Look, the two of you are a bit too emotional right now. Aryah, little

Lindsey betrayed us both but if I'm willing to put the past in the past so should you now let's all just calm down okay, I want us all to have a good time tonight, okay ladies, cut out the bullshit. Aryah, you get me tonight and as you can see, that's more than enough punishment for Lindsey!"

Lindsey apologizes to Aryah, and we finally get to the business at hand, pleasing me! We all get a couple lines and pop some X. The girls have finally loosened up after hitting the Skittles bowl and powdering their nose. Both are dancing and enjoying themselves. I mean, alcohol, coke and pills will turn the meanest bitch into little Ms. Sunshine. I duck off to the bedroom and grab the camcorder. I know that seems old school but there is no way I'm filming what's about to go down on my cellphone, my wife is too damn nosy. When I return, the girls have completely let go of their inhibitions. They're grinding on each other, touching and rubbing one another. One thing about these girls, it doesn't take a whole lot of coaxing to turn them into total fucking freaks. The alcohol and drugs help but that's what they do!

I put on my director's hat and ask them to remove each other's clothing. "Lindsey, take Aryah over to the sofa and do your thang baby." Whenever Lindsey hears, "do your thang", she knows to get on her knees. I set the recorder up directly across from the sofa to catch all the action. I can't let them have all the fun now, can I?

I quickly remove my clothing and sit next to Aryah. I suck her titties while Lindsey sucks and licks her pussy. We got this broad screaming and squirming at the same time. Once Aryah cums, I instruct Lindsey to lay flat on her back on the rug. "Aryah, get down there baby and play with that pussy a little for me. Aryah goes further, she pleasures Lindsey the same way. "Yeah, just like that baby." Aryah is soak and wet, so I easily slide in the pussy. I hit it for a couple minutes and pull out! I need to know if Aryah has "Top" game as good or better than Lindsey, she does not disappoint. Once I'm satisfied Aryah has mastered her "head game", I bend her over and begin pounding that fat ass. After several minutes, I hit the pussy again. I tried my hardest to pull out, but this bitch got some good pussy, I had to nut in it.

We all take a shower together and after a while, Lindsey comes down a bit from her high and she's upset with me. I ignore her and Aryah and I return to the living room to relax and listen to music. An hour goes by, and I dismiss Aryah with the promise to call her soon. I eventually go into the bedroom to check on Lindsey, feeling a slight tinge of guilt. She's crying hysterically and holding a white stick in her hand. Is this broad suicidal over a piece of pussy?

"What's the problem Lindsey," I ask beyond irritated. "I'm pregnant, again," she screams! What the hell?! "The fuck you mean you're pregnant?! Pregnant by who?! Whose baby are you carrying Lindsey and I know damn well you not trying to say me?!" She tries explaining to me that she used protection with Aryah's husband, and I must be the father. "Yo, I'm not trying to hear this bullshit, I know I'm not the father and I suggest you get rid of it like you did before! I got all the kids I want so don't think that I would leave my wife cause your stupid ass decided to get pregnant again. I'm outta here, fuck you and your baby bitch!" "Keenan, you can't leave me, and I can't have another abortion. I need you. I made a mistake with Aryah's husband, but I've been completely loyal to you outside of that. I can't kill another baby because you have this so-called perfect life. If you were that happy, you would have never been with me!" She's right but it doesn't change the fact that I don't want any outside kids. If my wife found this shit out, I would lose everything. "Lindsey, even if that baby is mine you can't have it, that could ruin me and then what, huh? You can't pay for this place, have you thought about that? I take care of you and now I'm telling you to take care of it or I'm out for good!" "I'm not killing another one of our babies Keenan so you're just going to have to figure it out, the baby is yours and I'm keeping our baby!" "Lindsey, you're making a mistake. I just hope it doesn't cost you more than you think," I reply calmly as I walk out the door. That shit just ruined my night! I had almost completely forgiven her, and she goes and drops a bomb! It doesn't matter if the baby's mine, there's no way I can think of before it's born to know for sure. Either way, I can't take a chance!

"Justin, what's up bro", sounding very animated at this point. "At the crib, what up Kee?" I explain to him the bullshit that just went down. "Man, get the fuck outta here, Kee, you got that bitch pregnant again bro? Man, you can't let that girl have your baby, hell is it your baby?" Justin seems more pissed about the situation than me, but he's my brother so I get it. "Aye, its gonna take me about twenty minutes to get home, can you meet me?" Of course, he agrees, and we end the call.

I'm still sitting in my car outside of Lindsey's when I decide to text Aryah about the pregnancy situation. I regret sending the text as soon as I hit send. I don't know this broad and used her for the purpose of hurting Lindsey, period! The phone rings, "Mando, its me Aryah." "Yeah, I know it's you, your name popped up!" "Mando, I'm so sorry, what are you going to do?" After explaining that I doubt I'm the father since she was screwing around, I'm not really concerned. "Actually baby girl, I was letting you know for obvious reasons. You could be a step mommy soon if she decides to keep it, but I don't want shit to do with Lindsey anymore. The bitch is too unstable. Look at all the shit she put into her system tonight. If she keeps the kid, it's probably gonna come out fucked up anyway," I exclaim! "You know she got pregnant on purpose, she takes the pill and if it's my husband's child, it's definitely over for us. I wasn't so sure I wanted to stay in the marriage after finding out about the two of them, right now, I'm undecided," Aryah retorts. We spend a couple more minutes on the phone reminiscing about the fun we did have tonight. Aryah is still on cloud nine, "I've never cheated on my husband with another man, but you were definitely worth it." "Aryah, when I came out of the bedroom, you and Lindsey were dancing and touching like you weren't just going at each other's throats an hour earlier, what's up with that," I question. "Well, when you have a close girlfriend and you party, things happen. Lindsey and I have had enjoyed one another on numerous occasions before we lost touch, it was a natural reaction for us both when you have party favors. She loves to eat my pussy and I love that she loves it," Aryah laughs. "So, tell me something Ms. Aryah, before tonight, you've never eaten Lindsey's pussy or any other woman," I question. Aryah responds, "no, I've never, I've played with a couple, and I've sucked breasts and kissed other women, but I've never gone as far as I did tonight. I went all the way there for you." I am a bit puzzled by that answer, so she goes deeper into why. "I wanted to prove to you that I'm a willing partner. You never have to worry that I'm going to trap you by becoming pregnant. You will never have to worry that I'm seeing someone else or that I want to replace your wife. I enjoy the company of a man of your caliber, that's it, that's all!" Now this is a sidepiece you keep around, it's over for Lindsey!

I finally arrive home and notice Justin and Mye are smiling and laughing while having a drink on the wrap around porch. I don't bother pulling into the garage and immediately jump out of the car. My boy better be just playing that role with my wife cause shit round here has gotten serious. Mye is in a pair of silk pajamas and she's glowing.

"What's up J," I ask with a sly smile, while winking at my wife and giving her soft kiss on the cheek. "Nothing much brother, just need to catch up with you before that trip." I agree and we all walk in the house before I excuse my "so called wife", the fuck out of our face and from my "man-cave" downstairs. I'm not sure why she's staring in confusion but my disdain for her is hard to hide. I have to find out what the hell she's doing, if anything at all!

"So, what the fuck up J, tell me something good man?" He sits down without responding with his hands over his head. At this point, I pour myself and him a drink cause I need to get down to the bottom of this bullshit before I go out of town. "Man, what's up, don't be sitting here holding yo fucking head when I'm asking you a simple ass question," I demand! After a few minutes pass without a word, he actually tells me that he hasn't done a damn thing I asked! "Look Kee, you going out of town tomorrow man. That's the perfect opportunity to catch anything that your woman might be doing if she's doing anything, and that's a big "if" brother! If you would focus on her ass more than these random bitches, you might not feel the way you're feeling, know what I'm saying?!" I can't get a word in edgewise as Justin continues. "You do so much dirty shit, you think this woman out here doing the same thing and its possible yo ass may just be wrong, And why the hell would you come home and hug all up on your wife knowing where you just came from? Brother, when you get that alcohol in you, you don't think clearly." I can't argue that fact at all. I know I'm a terrible husband when I got the best wife a man could ever ask for but I'm not thinking about that shit right now!

After some more back and forth I finally agree to let J wait until I leave. He leaves and I drink until I'm staggering and decide to keep my drunk ass downstairs for the night. My alarm blares at 5:30 the next morning and I'm feeling bad. I slowly make my way upstairs and head straight for the shower. I see Mye is still sleeping off whatever activities she had going on last night. It's a good thing, I had my bags packed last night cause the way I'm moving this morning, I will never make my flight! I've been waiting for this meeting for seven months after it was postponed this past winter due to inclement weather.

After a long hot shower, I step out into the bedroom to find my wife sitting up in bed and glaring at me. "What's wrong with you," I ask incredulously. "I'm just wondering what made you snap at me last night after giving me a hug and kiss, that's bipolar type shit," she responds. I was again reminding her that I was blowing up her phones, cell and work with no response. The more she tries to convince me that she was working and that was it, the more pissed I become. My wife thinks by walking her sexy ass over to me with nothing on and giving me a head job for the road that I'm supposed to forget about this, and I will, for now. I'm still angry but what man you know willing to turn down "top", swallow and all from their wife, none?!

We both head downstairs where the kids are already eating breakfast. "Good morning princes' and princesses," I exclaim! I must admit, even when I'm pissed at Mye, or fuck off just cause, I look at my kids and think, I've gotta do better as a man. Financially, I got it on lock, but stepping up to be a better man and role model for my sons, it has my conscientious churning, and the guilt has been mounting lately. We have a good breakfast, after I give my kids hugs and love and Mye walks with me out to the front. "Listen, I'll call you once I make it and check into the hotel. What is your day gonna look like," I ask curiously? "I don't have to be in court today, so I was thinking of working from home. Vic's actually coming over soon and were going to catch up on some pending cases and just hang out while the house is quiet, nothing earth shattering," she laughs. I smile, "well, if the two of you start drinking, turn the camera on and send it to me. I might need that after being in the bible belt for a week," I chuckle. "You're a pig," Mye yells, kisses me lovingly, walks away and slams the door behind her.

My driver grabs my bags, tosses them in the back and we're off. The drive to the airport is normally about thirty minutes but traffic is a bit heavy this morning but flying private allows you to skip those long lines. I arrive forty-five minutes later where Shapiro has his private jet waiting. I can't deny, I like the way Shapiro is already trying to woo me! The flight is less than two hours, and they have champagne, fresh fruit and his personal stewardess comes out with a nice prime rib, scrambled eggs and waffles. "Mr. Washington," she asks, "would you care for a drink after your breakfast? Mr. Shapiro suggested Hennessey for you," she smiles. "Sure, after we're in the air and I chow down on this breakfast you all have prepared Ms.," I question. "It's Valencia Mr. Washington," she smiles again and walks away. After a couple minutes, she back with my orange juice and states there's a slight delay so I'll have ample time for breakfast and a drink and to just relax. After finishing breakfast, I recline my seat, close my eyes and do just that, relax.

So many things are running through my head, Lindsey's pregnant, I wanna see Aryah and Memphis would be the perfect spot. No one knows either of us, just two people from out of town enjoying the sites. I want to know what's going on with my wife, but Justin is right, there's probably nothing to it and I'm just paranoid. I try to clear my mind of everything as Valencia struts back in. I have to admit, I'm surprised a white man of Shapiro's status would have a personal black flight attendant. She's a beautiful woman, cocoa brown skin and thick, her titties could be bigger, but she got ass for days. "Mr. Washington, would you like along with your drink?" I nod yes and she opens a gold box sitting atop a beautiful Italian marble table and brings over the cigar, lighter and ashtray. Valencia explains our flight will be taking off in half hour or so.

After several minutes in the air, I ask Valencia to make me another drink. I'm not a fan off flying, although I have to often for work and when I do, I need Hennessey to get through it! After having a couple drinks, I head to the bathroom to get my bearings. Now that I've eaten, had some Hen, and we're sailing through the Midwestern skies, I'm feeling pretty good. Valencia returns and informs me that we will be landing in a little over an hour. Damn, I think to myself! I feel like we should have already been there, must be the anxiety I get when flying. When I enquire, Valencia states that Mr. Shapiro instructed his pilot to fly over downtown Chicago on the way because he knows that's originally where I'm from. Nice, I think to myself. The man has thought of everything thus far!

We finally land and Valencia informs me that a driver will take me to the Peabody, downtown Memphis and I should contact the driver once I've settled in. I'm a bit perplexed as I recall our meeting is scheduled for 2pm sharp. Valencia explains that I can contact Mr. Shapiro once I'm in the car. "There's a phone in the back with a direct line to Mr. Shapiro," she explains, just pick up the receiver and you will reach him. I hope you enjoyed your flight and look forward to seeing you for your return home Mr. Washington." With that, Valencia, pilot and co-pilot drive off together.

I jump into back of an extended Cadillac SUV and notice this man literally has a standing phone in his vehicle! who has a phone in their personal vehicle anymore? "Wow," I exclaim, I really didn't think these existed anymore, guess I wrong! I slowly pick up the receiver, still not believing anyone would be on the other end and I hear, "Mr. Washington, how was your flight?" "It was great, nice and smooth and thanks so much for the flyover, nothing like the magnificent mile when the sun's out!" We talk for a couple of minutes as the driver rolls toward downtown and Shapiro explains that today won't be as formal as I initially thought. With that, we end the call and I sit back and relax for the rest of ride.

Getting to the was non-eventful. There were no traffic delays like the ones I'm used to back home. We arrive at the hotel and guest services have two young brothers in suits rocking some long dreads ready to take my bags upstairs. I think to myself, it's good to be in a predominately "chocolate city". They greet me and we arrive at the seventh floor, enter my suite and I pass both some cash as they leave. I relax on a chaise lounge for a while just staring out at the sites as far as my eyes can see.

"Hey, what's up baby," I say to MyeZelle. "Hey honey, how was your flight," she asks. I give her the rundown on my trip and how it was a bit longer because Brad's pilot flew me over Chicago. We go over what was supposed to be my schedule for today and let her know once I'm back at the hotel, I'll check back in with her and the kids.

After showering and dressing into a two-piece suit with a button down, open collar, a pair of Gators, I'm ready to head to the lobby. I stop in the bar for a double shot, call Brad and await his driver. He arrives a short time later and informs me that we are headed over to a place on Beale Street, Club 152. I'm thinking, why are we going to a bar in the middle of the afternoon and who's going to be there this time of day wondering if it's a strip club as I laugh aloud.

It takes less than five minutes to arrive and Mr. Shapiro is standing outside with his pearly whites on full display. "Since we aren't discussing formal business right now Keenan, let's take a walk upstairs, shall we?" There's literally no crowd to be found, only staff but it's early. We make our way to the third floor. I see a couple guys in the VIP area, relaxing, having drinks. As we walk over, Brad assures me, "Mr. Washington, Keenan can I call you Kennan being that we're far from a board room?" I'm amused, yet appreciate the respect at the same time, "hey man, we're all good. I can adapt to any situation, just don't put on any Elvis, alright," I laugh boisterously. I continue to smile as we grab seats across from the other guys. After a brief introduction, we sit back enjoy some drinks, small banter and the sounds of Hov, Kendrick Lamar, Ye and T.I. I guess they think that's all I listen to. My best friend is of the Caucasian persuasion, and I consider myself a well-rounded guy with an uncanny ability to blend with people from any background but Shapiro's obviously trying to pull out all the stops which is great for Justin and me.

We sip drinks and enjoy the music but I'm already feeling the affects of the plane ride and the alcohol. "Alright Brad, you want to tell me exactly why I'm in Memphis. I mean this is cool and all but I'm here for business, so what's up?" After a brief pause in the music, we spend the next three hours discussing business, what Brad sees as a takeover. I can't deny, what I'm hearing sounds exactly like what I've been striving for my entire life. Shapiro has a great vision into what will be a very lucrative partnership.

The other guys depart, and we continue to discuss Brad's vision. He's secured the contract for a new Fed Ex hub here in Memphis along with contracts for a hundred new homes in a new development in a suburb of Memphis. The only downside to all of this, I would have to relocate, at least temporarily to Memphis and I don't see MyeZelle going for this at all. "Brad, I have to tell you, everything sounds great, perfect but I have a wife and four children who are settled in Minneapolis life as it is. My partner, Justin may be all for it, I just don't know if that's something I can commit to. I don't see my wife uprooting our family and her practice to make this happen." "Look Keenan, I know it's a lot to take in right now but what we're offering you is going make you known not just in the North and the East Coast. If we make this deal, once the project is over, it's L.A. baby, the west coast."

We make plans for the official meeting tomorrow at ten and I return to the hotel. "Hey baby, what's going on," I ask my wife. I briefly tell her what's happening here and she's not happy at all. "I don't understand Kee. We live hundreds of miles from Memphis. How is that going to work? Do you understand that you will be away from me and the kids, what one year, two years?" "I know MyeZelle but if you would stop running your mouth for just a minute and listen, I have a plan A & B depending on which one you're feeling. Plan A, we all move here for two years, the kids can think of it as an extended vacation. Plan B, you and the kids continue as you are, I rent an apartment or condo here and fly in every other weekend," I plead and hold my breath for MyeZelle's comeback. "You can't take this job Kee, we need you here with us," MyeZelle shouts! Everything I say is going in one ear and out the other. "Damn woman, if you would just hear me out, you would see the bigger picture! Do you realize how much money is out there in L.A., Las Vegas, just California alone?! That's where the money is, that's where we need to be! All of that can happen once I complete the contracts here in Memphis Mye. It's two years max, that's going to go by faster than you're imagining right now. We can do this together and I need you to believe in me baby!" Mye has been radio silent for over a minute, I digress. "Look, let's not make this decision tonight, we're both too amped up, okay baby, just get some sleep and we'll talk tomorrow," I plead. Mye isn't having it and she's giving me a damn headache. I hang up minus a promise my wife would, at minimum, think about the proposal. At the end of the day, MyeZelle will have to compromise because I'm taking the job. Now, I just have to figure out a way to get her stubborn ass on board!

MyeZelle

After getting the kids off to school, I give Vic a call to find out what time she's coming over. "I'm on my way and just so you know, I'm really pissed at you! I'll be there in half an hour." With that, she hangs up on me. I smile to myself thinking Vic is so damn dramatic! "Rose, will you whip something up for Victoria and I to eat while we're working please." "Of course, Mrs. M, what would like?" "I don't know, maybe turkey sub sandwiches and a fruit tray, something light, thanks Rose!"

I head downstairs to the family room and set up my laptop to get started on a new case involving a professional basketball player who happens to be married and now is being blackmailed by a woman claiming he's fathered her "love child". I'll never understand why these superstar athletes won't at least strap up when they're screwing around with these groupie hoes! Just as I'm finishing a cease-and-desist letter, my phone rings, it Ron! "Hello." "What's up baby, how's your day going?" I explain that I'm working from home today but I'm really busy and don't have time to talk. "Listen, I need to see you tonight, can you stop by the club?" "I can't Ron, I'm sorry. My husband is out of town and Vic is on her way over so we can go over some cases. I have to be here when my children get home and there's no way I can leave." "MyeZelle, I need to see you tonight, I'm going through something, and I need you baby, please!" I know that I shouldn't give in to Ron but fuck it! "I don't know what time it's going to be. I have to be home when my kids arrive, check their homework, have dinner and make sure everyone has showered and ready for bed." Ron sighs and I'm hoping, praying that he will give me a rain check because I want to see this man again, just not tonight. "Sweetheart, whatever time you can make it, I'll be here waiting." With that we end the call.

A short time later, I hear the doorbell and assume its Victoria. "Hey hoe," she laughs. I smile, "I'm not a hoe, I just got caught up in the moment, but its over now." "Girl, that man is in love with you and if you think, he's just going to go away and that's that, you really are crazy!" Again, I lie, "well, he's gonna have to get over it because what he wants, I can't give him," exasperated by Vic's interest in Ron, I finally decide to say "fuck it", and tell Victoria everything.

Starting with the fact Ron's bought this penthouse downtown, set it up for me and the kids and she's in shock. "MyeZelle, this sounds like some fatal attraction type shit. What are you going to do and what happens if Keenan finds out? He's going to kill you! Do you care about Ron?" "I mean, yeah, he's a really good guy and the sex is incredible, amazing even! I can't put into words just how amazing he is. I don't know why he's not married. Shit, if I wasn't married, he wouldn't have to worry about chasing me because I'd be on him like white on rice." I tell Vic how Ron is pleading for me to see him tonight. "I don't know how you're going to do it but whatever you do, be careful. And after the conversation you overheard, clearly he's planning on hiring a private investigator or someone follow you MyeZelle. With him out of town, it wouldn't surprise me if he has Justin's ass sniffing around like the dog that he is," she laughs. "Yeah, I know Vic alright, and trust me I'm going to be very careful! Men don't know how to cover their tracks versus women, I got this. Can we please get to work now?"

Vic and I spend the next four hours discussing clients, typing motions and responses. "I need a drink, what about you?" "Sure, why not. I'm pretty much done for day. So, are you going to Ron's tonight?" "I don't know Vic, he didn't really leave me a choice. I don't want him showing up to my home again. Speaking of, we never figured out how Ron got my address in the first place?" Vic looks at me puzzled. "I'm not sure Mye but the fact that he knows where you live and is demanding to see you is scary. Messing around on your husband is one thing but you've gotten yourself into some real bullshit this time MyeZelle and I don't know how to help you. I know he seems to be a great guy but clearly he's in love, possibly obsessed and could turn into a fatal attraction." She hugs me and I burst into tears, crying uncontrollably. "What am I supposed to do Vic, my husband has been living the single life throughout our marriage. He has been having his cake and eating it too for years! Ignoring my wants and needs as a wife and I've tried to communicate my feelings to Keenan, but he doesn't give a damn. I want to be loved, really and wholly loved like anyone else. Honestly, I'm not sure I love Kee enough anymore to fight for this marriage. I know a divorce might hurt my kids but it's not working for me anymore and I know they can see that as well, especially our boys. I don't want them to grow up thinking the way Keenan treats me is how you're supposed to treat your wife or girlfriend, you know?" Victoria nods her head in agreement but remain silent as I continue to pour my heart out.

"The truth is, I want to see him. Ron makes me feel alive again and now Keenan is talking about this deal in Memphis, it could be the perfect opportunity for me to find out if this is something I really want to pursue. Kee and I had a conversation about the move last night and I was initially against it because there's no way in hell I'm moving my children to the south but I will be more than happy for him to go. He would have to move there for maybe two years, traveling back and forth." "Mye, I'm all for you and my godchildren being happy and whatever is best for you and the kids, I'm all for. All I ask is that you are extra careful with whatever you do and don't get dick crazy over this guy to the point where you forget you are still a married woman!" "I could go with you to make things look better, if Keenan really is having you watched. Everyone knows you don't go out anywhere unless you're with me or Keenan. "No,

I don't need you to go Vic, I'll be fine," I reassure Victoria. I get myself together and decide to give Ron a call back after Vic leaves.

"Hey, I was just calling because I'm really tired Ron, I've had a rough day. Can we meet for lunch tomorrow?" He declines, "baby girl, I need to see you tonight, please Mye, just come by. I won't keep you out all night, I promise." I finally agree and let him know that I'll be there once my kids arrive home from school, enjoy dinner together and get them settled in for the night.

"Hey momma, the girls say in unison. "Hey my beautiful ones, how was school?" Kendra goes first, "the usual momma, same boring stuff. I'm so glad its only two weeks left before summer break. Momma, where are we going on vacation this year? I want to go back to Disney World momma." Kenya buts in, "no momma, can we go somewhere else? Why does Kendra get to pick where we go anyway?" I explain to both their dad, and I haven't decided where we're going on vacation this year and when we do, they will be the first to know. "Alright girls let's get homework done, so we can have dinner soon. Are your brothers home yet?" "Yes ma'am," they again say in unison.

I make my way to the family room where the twins, of course, are playing Fortnite. "Guys, has homework been taken care of because its dinner time. Lasagna, salad, bread sticks and dessert, let's go!" Of course, my boys fall right in line, but my girls are more hyper. "Let's go little ladies," I say, a bit agitated at the slower pace my children seem to be moving tonight. It could be my anxiety is on twelve with thoughts of seeing Ron tonight.

After dinner, we spend some time watching TV and facetime with Keenan. From the outside looking in, one would think we really have perfect family. Keenan is capable of portraying that that image to my children and our social circle so well, it's almost impossible to fathom him being anything other.

I put my thoughts in my pocket and get prepared to meet Ron. First things first, I need to play with my pussy so I don't have to crave this man tonight. I get dressed in a simple Fendi mini dress and matching pumps to head out the door. As I'm backing out of the garage, I see a familiar car, its Justin's ass! What in the world is he doing here? I jump out to find out what's going on, "hey what's up Justin," I ask irritated. "Nothing much lady, I was just stopping by to check on you guys since Keenan's out of town, that's all. Where are you going looking like that," he questions. I respond by telling him one, it's not his business but if he's so interested, he's more than welcome to join Vic and I for a drink. Justin just laughs and says, "nah sis, I'm good. I only came by to make sure y'all were straight. It's all good, be careful, you and Vic have a goodnight." With that, Justin gets back in his car and drives off and I do the same.

Once I arrive to Ron's main club downtown, I give him a quick call to let him know I'm downstairs. Normally, I'm greeted by one of his "guys" but its Ron instead. I cannot describe enough times or ways just how fucking fine this man is more than I have already. He can literally put anything on, other than skinny jeans and be the sexist man alive, outside of DeZe, Denzel that is, who needs no last name!

"Hey sweetheart, how are," he asks very softly. This is the type of bullshit that makes me crave him more and more. "Hey, I'm here, so what's the big emergency?" "Sweetheart, walk upstairs with me and just indulge me for a while. I know a lot of brothers don't usually do shit like this, at least nobody I know anyway. I'm trying to do something, just work with me, alright?" I oblige, and allow him to walk me upstairs, so I thought. Where he takes me, is not his "love nest" upstairs but the VIP of the club where he normally watches the crowd and relax. "Ron, will you tell me exactly why I'm here?" Instead of answering my question he just stares at me. A feeling of dread along with fear washes over me and I to walk away. "Come back and sit down for a minute, I need to talk to you. I don't want you to be afraid of me MyeZelle. I told you, I would never hurt you or put you in any danger. If I thought for one second you would be in any real danger, I wouldn't pursue you. I'll never let him hurt you. I think you know how I can get down if I need to and dude not about that life, you don't have nothing to worry about with me." After a couple drinks, light conversation and "people watching", Ron pulls me into his arms, and we stay that way for some time before I fall asleep.

I awake to Ron carrying me upstairs, the first place we made love. "Mye, I didn't ask you to come here to get you back in my bed, I just want to spend some time with you and chill. You can stay here and rest a couple hours, you seem tired but if you're up for it, there's something in the bathroom for you. Put it on and meet me in the "SVIP." I look at him confused, "what do you mean SVIP? I've only been to one VIP, is there another," I ask confused. "I'm sorry baby, my bad, it's a new spot I added separate from VIP. It's a little more private, cozy, not a lot of room for others." He notices the look on my face and says, "MyeZelle, don't worry, I'm not gonna make love to you in front of three hundred people, unless you want me to, they wouldn't be able to see us anyway," he laughs. "Baby, just call me when you're ready and I'll come get you okay?" He kisses me on the forehead and leaves.

I begrudgingly walk over to the bathroom and Ron has not one fit for me to pick out but three! What the hell does this man think, "I'm his own personal human black barbie," I exclaim aloud! I'm feeling very insecure and a bit agitated! "Ron," I yell into my cell, "what the hell do you think this is? I came here looking forward to spending time with you and you want me to play dress up? I don't know what you're thinking but I'm out!" With that I hang up, exit the bathroom, grab my purse and await the elevator.

The doors open and there is Ron with the biggest smile on his face, "damn baby, why you gotta be so mean? I just want to see you in something no one else has! I'm not knocking the way you dress, that's the shit that turned me on in the first place. Mye, you got a body better than any dancer at my clubs. You should be showing that shit twenty-four/seven!" I unleash my anger and try, once again, to explain to this asshole, one I'm a wife and mother. Two, I'm a lawyer, not a fucking stripper, three, and most important, I'm a grown ass woman capable of picking my wardrobe out without his help! It's like I'm talking to a brick wall. After more than twenty minutes of a back and forth at the elevator, we re-enter the bedroom to debate more!

After I calm down, I realize why Ron wants to see me in something no one, including my husband has ever seen me in. I guess, if I was a man, I would feel the same way. We kiss and I go back into the bathroom to decide what would turn him on the most tonight. I decide on a striped jumper with sheer siding and clear five-inch heels. Once dressed, I unpin my hair and do light touchup on face and head back to the elevator. "Hey, I'm on my way down," I say nervously to Ron.

He's waiting as I exit the elevator and the look on his face says it all! I have to admit, it's really nice to have a man look at a woman the way Ron looks at me. It's as if each time he sees me, it's for the very first time. "Wow, baby if you were candy, I would literally die of diabetes," he screams in excitement! I laugh and he holds my hand and walks me pass VIP to this "SVIP", whatever that is.

As we walk through the glass doors, I notice the delicate colors, everything is decorated in a soft pink or tea rose. We sit on a plush two-seater, rose and teal color chaise lounge. He has candles everywhere. There's a soft scent of lavender in the air. "So Mye, the "SVIP" is, she's a very important person. I cut off a section of the main VIP room to add this just for you. I had my guys surround it in six inch thick glass walls so the music isn't so deafening. Can you tell the difference?" I nod my head and smile. "It's absolutely amazing Ron, its beautiful. You have great taste in everything. You're very thoughtful but we've had this conversation more than once. I don't need you to spoil me, I can do that myself." He holds his finger to his lips essentially hushing me.

Minutes pass and he picks up a landline phone next to him. "Baby, what do want to drink," he asks. I respond, "I'll have a Rob Roy, thanks." Ron looks at me quizzically, shakes his head and orders our drinks. A Rob Roy is simply a scotch with hints of fruit and vanilla flavors, topped with an orange slice and maraschino cherries. It also gives an instant mellowness that a single puff of a blunt would do for someone like me who's not true smoker.

Once our drinks arrive, we spend the next couple of hours watching the crowd below and listening to old and new school r & b. I check the time and its close to 11 o'clock. I turn to Ron and before I can speak, he kisses me lovingly. It's as if our tongues are slow dancing to H.E.R. featuring Chris Brown's new song "come Through." I find it increasingly difficult to describe how this man makes feel. There's this pain that surges through my pelvis when he touches me. His hands are so warm as if he has a fever. I can feel the heat on my thigh as he rubs them. "Ron, its late, I really need to get home." His eyes are so sad, they're saying, "I'm never going to see her again." "Ron, I have to go honey, I have to be home when my kids wake up." I should have kept that part to myself because as usual, he has an answer for everything. "I'll make sure you're at home before the sun comes up. They'll never know you weren't there. Please Mye, stay with me a little while longer baby, I need you tonight, I really do." We spend another hour or so with me wanting to leave and him begging me to stay. Shortly after midnight, he calls his bottle girls and instructs them to set us up with drinks in his private bedroom. "Look, I gotta run downstairs to handle a couple things, I'll see you up there in a little bit." With that, he goes down and I head up.

The sounds of Childish Gambino or Donald Glover as he prefers to be called lately fills the room. I undress apart from my thong and help myself to another drink. At this point I'm not feeling any guilt of being away from home. I mean, hell, who knows what Keenan is doing in Memphis right now. If I was a betting woman, it would bet he's with some white trash country bumpkin tramp with big tits and "noassatall"!

Ron enters the private suite a short time later. He immediately undresses down to his wife beater tee and boxers. Dear God, this is one sexy black man! His physique, walk, smile and everything about him gives my entire body shivers. "What's up baby girl, you alright," he asks. I smile and nod yes as he leans down to lift my chin up for another passionate kiss. I moan just a little to assure him I want him just as much as he wants me. I watch in awe as he removes his Ethika briefs, like "The Game" has worn on Instagram, is all the enticement I need. A man with a great body and very well endowed can get away with wearing Ethika briefs, and Ron can give "The Game" a run for his money in that and many other departments. He slides in next to me and adjusts the bed where we are sitting upright, and our legs are in a bended position. Reaching over to his left, Ron grabs this insane gaming like gadget and start pressing buttons. Suddenly the music stops, a screen drops from the ceiling, and he asks in the most sexy, husky whisper, "can we watch a movie, is that okay baby?" "Sure," I respond, "that sounds nice." He hits play and I immediately recognize the intro music, its "50 Shades of Grey", not the latest sequel to come out but the original. "What made you pick this movie Ron," I hesitantly ask. He just smiles and explains he's not deep into S & M but he would like to make me immobile just to see how my body responds. I would normally object to this but the way he describes it sounds so erotic. With more detail and assurances, I agree to experiment.

After my wrists are tied to the bed, my legs are pulled clamped in an upward position as if I'm ready to do crunches, only I can't release them if I wanted to. He asks if I'm ready and immediately lifts my hips to slide my thong down my thighs and over my knees to the clamps holding my ankles. Crawling back up towards me, he runs his hand up my thigh, spreads my lips and starts fingering my wet pussy. I begin to moan and beg for him to just, "please fuck me already baby, please," I beg. He ignores me and continues finger fucking me with one hand, caressing and plucking my hard nipple with the other and yelling for me to say how much I want him. When I refuse, Ron gets up from the bed and just stares at me. "What are you doing, why did you stop honey?" I ask, in disbelief that he just pulled this shit! "I want you to say you want me but if you don't, I'll untie you and drive you home. Do you want me MyeZelle?" Horny and angry at this point, I tell him, "fine, take me home Ron, I don't have time for this shit!" He obliges and disgusted with him and myself at this point, I hurry to the bathroom to change into my clothes and prepare to leave. But, for some reason, I can't walk out of this damn bathroom! I'm balling at this point as Ron walks in and holds me. "Do you want me MyeZelle," he again asks. "Ron, I can't," I respond. "If you don't want me, why are you still here," with that Ron walks out of the bathroom, readjusts the bed to a normal sleep position and lays there. Everything in me is telling me this is my chance to get away from him for good, but my legs won't move. "Ron," I whisper. "MyeZelle, I don't want to play games with you no more, if you want to leave, leave! I'm not getting ready to keep chasing you!" Ron redresses as I'm hysterically crying and can't stop. He totally ignores me and walks out the door. I disappear back into the bathroom and cry until I'm all cried out. I look in the mirror and my face is completely flushed, my eyes are bloodshot with bags underneath. It was all the excuse I needed to get undressed, climb back in this man's bed and wait for him, damn it, I do want him and I'm over denying myself pleasures I've been missing for so long in my marriage!

After waiting over an hour for Ron to return, I eventually fall asleep. I have no idea when he decided to show up, but the movie was over. I could feel his warm naked body pressed against mine and I felt so safe. Just before dawn, Ron wakes me up and I quickly dress and prepare to head home. "You slept like a baby MyeZelle. You were snoring," he chuckles. I giggle a bit and agree to come back tonight after I put my kids to bed. Ron walks me out to my car, gives me a quick kiss and with that, I head for home.

꧁ Justin

I already know I'm wasting my time but I decided to drive my wife's car and park down the street from Keenan and MyeZelle's home. Once I saw her drive off, I raced home, switched cars and was back in less than forty-five minutes. Either she changed her mind about going out with Vic or Ms. MyeZelle has been out all night! The innocent explanation is she and Vic got fucked up last night and they crashed at Victoria's place downtown. MyeZelle just doesn't seem like the type of woman to add undue bullshit to her life, the woman's already wound too tight!

As I'm gathering my thoughts, I see MyeZelle rolling down the street before turning into their garage. Damn, so she did stay out all night but it doesn't mean she was with another man, so I won't jump to conclusions just yet. I'm also not telling Keenan at this point. There's no need to get him all hyped if the situation turns out to be nothing. I pull into their driveway before MyeZelle has a chance to close the garage door. "Good morning Mrs. Washington," I announce somewhat sarcastically! "Justin, what are you doing here this time of morning," she demands! I lie, "me and my wife got into another bad fight, I didn't want to go to a hotel, and I didn't want to wake you up, so I took her car. I figured the safest place for me to get a little sleep was to park on y'all street. I can make sure everything was good here and get a couple hours of sleep at the same time." "I'm not sure sleeping in your car is protecting me and my kids! And you can tell Kee that I know he's trying to have me followed and the shit isn't going to work! He's wasting his, yours and my time because I'm not doing a damn thing unless he considers sleeping at my best friend's house after too many drinks is a crime!" How in the hell does she know Kee wants me to follow her, I wonder! MyeZelle is furious and she makes sure I know just how pissed she really is. "You can tell your boss to not worry about what I'm doing and instead try to make sure his dick doesn't fall off from screwing every nasty white bitch that throws the pussy at him and do remember to tell him I keep my heat on me so for anyone following me, I may fear for my life and just start shooting!"

MyeZelle immediately turns away meaning she has spoken, and I am not worthy of anymore of her time. Damn that woman is mean! I understand why she's so sought after as an attorney, she shut my ass up quick! After walking back to my car, tail between my legs, I decide not to call Keenan. I really don't believe MyeZelle would cheat on my brother and with the tongue lashing I had just been given, I figure it's better not to ever mention this fiasco of a covert operation I tried pulling off to anyone!

Once I make it home, I'm greeted by yet another angry ass woman! My wife didn't wait for me to close the door before going straight in. "So, which one of your whores have you been entertaining this time Justin?! I am so fed up with you pretending to be a single man when clearly you are not! I'm filing for divorce, it's over," she screams! I hadn't noticed she was fully dresses until she snatched her set of keys from my hand and stormed out the door. Divorce, great! One less bitch I have to deal with. After getting undressed and taking a quick shower, I crawl into bed and allow my mind to replay the events of last night into this morning. All hasn't been lost as long as Carrina sticks to her guns and give me a divorce, laughing to myself.

Thinking a bit further, I can use that as another excuse for MyeZelle. The approach would be, I really needed to talk to her if Carrina decides to follow through on her threat of a divorce. Explain to her the need to protect my assets and get it over with as quickly as possible. MyeZelle knows I don't give a damn about the marriage, but I'll do anything to keep all my money and properties. After getting the new plan together, I fall asleep just before 10:30 in the morning.

⟡ MyeZelle

I can't believe this bastard, my husband had Justin watching me! Is he crazy?! Clearly Keenan doesn't understand his mistrust for me stems from his years of infidelity. I now know exactly who he was talking to, and I now know how to handle the situation.

I slip into the house and of course Rosie is in the kitchen busy as usual. "Good morning", she smiles brightly. "Good morning Rosie, are the kids still sleeping", I ask nervously. "Yes ma'am, they have about thirty minutes before waking. You have time to change and climb in bed." Sensing Rosie's suggestion was more of a plea considering the clothes I'm still wearing, I give her a slight smile, nod and heed her advice.

I climb into bed and the only thing on my mind is Ron. I want this man badly. I'm craving him like a pregnant woman craves pickles! Just as I'm thinking of Ron, my phone rings and it's Ron! "Hello," I answer. "Hey sweetheart, I wanted to give you time to make it home and settle in, are you alright?" "Yes honey, I'm fine, I'm home." He laughs and responds, "So are you coming back to see me after you get the babies off to school?" Before I can respond, Ron continues. "Tell me something MyeZelle, were you thinking about me before I called? Is my pussy still throbbing baby? You want daddy to bust it open since I didn't last night?" Ron waits for a response but I'm speechless because I can't deny, that's exactly what I want him to do. "I have to help get my kids dressed, down for breakfast and out the door, can I call you later?" "Not unless you're meeting me at home, our penthouse. You remember where it is right?" "Yes, I know where it is Ron but…" "Look," Ron cuts me off. "I'm headed to the penthouse; I'll leave your set of keys with the front desk. I'll be waiting for you MyeZelle." Ron doesn't give me a chance to rebuff his demand before ending the call. I mean, sure, I would have tried to convince him there was no way I could see him today but the truth is, I'm glad he hung up because I do want to see him!

Leaping out of bed, I dance to the bathroom to freshen up and go in search of the troops to make sure they're on schedule.

After enjoying breakfast with the troops and having a short talk with Rosie, I skip upstairs to dress for work. Although I will be in the downtown area, I have little if no intentions at all of showing up to the office today. Once I'm "work ready" I head back downstairs to give Rosie an update on my schedule for the day. "Rosie, I will need you to fill in for me this evening as I have a late dinner meeting after court. You can always call if you or the kids need me." "No, Mrs. M, we will be fine. Enjoy your day and good luck at your dinner meeting. I hope it goes well," Rosie replies with a sincere smile. "I'm sure it will Rosie. Thanks again!"

I arrive less than twenty minutes later to Ron's building. As I approach the front desk, I'm greeted by a handsome young Italian man. "Good morning Mrs. Henderson, your husband left your keys for you." "Excuse me," I reply in astonishment! "Mr. Henderson brought your house keys down this morning ma'am. He said you forgot them and showed me a photo so I would know who you are, I'm sorry I thought he would have spoken to you." I go along with the shenanigans Ron is throwing my way. "I'm sorry my mind is a million miles away, thank you and your name is so I'll know who you are next time?" "Of course, I'm Gabriel. I always work the morning shift 6-6 so if you or your husband need anything, please don't hesitate to ring me. I'll also need your keys to have our runner bring your car into your private parking space. Your keys will be left in your center console for you." Without objection, we trade keys and I make my way toward the elevators to my "other" home.

My keys work perfectly and as I enter, I can hear a slight noise from down the hall, likely coming from the master bedroom. After kicking off my hills and placing my purse and new keys on the credenza to the right of me, I quietly make my way to the master bedroom. Ronald is sleeping to the sounds of Sports Center as I enter and without waking him, I strip down to nothing and slowly climb in bed next to him. Without missing a beat Ron grabs me in his arms and kisses me passionately. The longer our tongues dance, the hotter and wetter I become. He turns his attention to my breasts and my nipples come alive. Ron has one hand holding my left breast while our tongues continue to dance, he uses his other hand to gently massage my wet pussy. As I begin to moan, he slowly makes his way down to his prize. Ron rids us of the down comforter and spreads my legs. "Grab your legs baby and hold them for me, don't let go", he demands! I comply in anticipation of what's to come. Ron spreads my lips apart and tongues my clit until I scream in ecstasy. I allow my legs to fall but Ron insists I keep them up. I again do as I'm instructed, and Ron repeats the tongue kiss on my clit. After shaking uncontrollably, he allows me to let go. He thrusts himself inside me and tears begin to fall from my face. I've fallen in love with this man, and I know it's going to create a storm. Ron notices my tears and we take a break. "Sweetheart, what's wrong, was I too rough," he asks. "No, everything is right, everything feels right, and we both know it's wrong. I'm falling in love with you Ron and I have no idea how to handle it or how to deal with it." "Baby, you don't have to deal with anything. I told you, your husband isn't about that life. Whenever you want to leave, you have a home right here with me." I don't respond and Ron doesn't add anymore, he just holds me until we both fall sleep.

Hours pass when I'm awaken by the constant ringing of a cell phone and Ron's strong voice. "If she wanted you to know where she was, she would have told yo ass and I'm not your client so you shouldn't be calling my phone at all but yeah, she's with me and she's going to be with me" he yells and hangs up his phone. My nerves are shaken to the core. "Ron, who was that, was that my husband?!" "No sweetheart that was Victoria. Look, she knows what time it is. That's your girl, she's not gonna turn on you. Her ass just mad she doesn't have a real one like me giving her anything she wants and busting that pussy out," he laughs. "I didn't call her to let her know that I wouldn't be in the office today. After getting the kids off to school, I came straight here, to you." "That's what you're supposed to do, come home to me. You own that practice and brought her ass along for the ride so she better be grateful!" "Can you give me something to throw on please, I need to grab my phone from my purse," concerned about Vic's state of mind at this point. "Why would you need to put on clothes in your own home, our home," Ron retorts! He continues, "sweetheart, you stay right here, I'll bring it to you. The kids are in school, your ex-husband is hundreds of miles away and you don't punch a clock so relax." Ron walks away before I can respond. This man just called my husband, my ex!

"Sweetheart, I'm running to grab us something to eat cause you don't look like you have any energy left to cook", he laughs. He's right, I'm totally drained physically and exhausted mentally! Once Ron leaves, I have the opportunity to call Victoria back, something I clearly regret now! "Hey Vic, what's going on," I ask in a shaky voice. Victoria wastes no time getting straight to the point. "MyeZelle, I'm not going to yell at you because that's pointless. I get the fact that your husband ain't shit and you deserve to feel good, but you do understand that Keenen hasn't moved to Memphis or even decided to take the job yet? You need to be very careful." "I will Vic, I promise, I have so much to tell you. Rosie is taking care of the kids tonight. Can you come over?" There's a long pause before Vic responds, "you want me to come over to Ron's house after the way he spoke to me earlier on the phone, are you fucking kidding me Mye?" I beg Vic to trust me enough to come over after she leaves the office, she finally agrees.

Ron makes it back with our late lunch/early dinner from Panera Bread. "So, I grabbed enough to give you some energy for round two," with a mischievous smile. "We have Autumn Squash soup, a greek salad and steak and arugula on panini." "Ron, I can't eat all of this and I need to talk with you about something." "Oh shit, here we go again, now what MyeZelle? You can't see me anymore, what now," he demands! "Will you please calm down, it's nothing like what you're thinking!" After Ron calms down, I explain to him that Victoria and I talked, I invited her over so that I can explain everything to her and she agreed without any anger. "Alright sweetheart, if you think that's a good idea, I'm fine with it, I mean this is your home and I will do whatever it takes to make you happy. I'll even apologize for going in on Victoria if that's what you want, okay? Now, can I go grab the dinner trays so we can eat, please," walking away!

After our meal, Ron decides it's better if he's not here, just in case Vic's other personality comes out. "You know your girl is bat shit crazy right baby? I mean I don't mind apologizing but no one gets that wound up over their best friend fucking another man unless you're fucking her too!" "Is that supposed to be a question Ron? I need to take a shower before Vic gets here." As I walk towards the bathroom, Ron gently grabs my arm, "do you and Vic have something going on baby, be honest with me." "No Ron we don't, Vic and I had some crazy college days together like many other young women but we are strictly best friends and business partners now and that's it okay. I need to take a hot shower and you need to disappear before she gets here," I yell! "Alright sweetheart, damn you mean when you want to be," smiling from ear to ear! "I'll be down the street at the club, call me and let me know what you want for dinner. You are staying right?" "Yes, Ron I'm staying but I have to work tomorrow, and I have to go home at least until my children fall asleep so everything seems normal. And I have to take calls from my husband, if he calls," I explain along with a sigh. Ron grabs my waist and holds me so tightly, it takes my breath away. He whispers softly in my ear, "I'm in love with you and I'm gonna make you my wife." Without allowing me to respond, he kisses me softly on the lips, neck, walks to the bedroom door and disappears down the hallway.

After a hot shower, I check the walk-in closet Ron has filled with clothing and shoes for me. I find animal print lounge pj's with matching slippers. As I'm getting dressed my cell is ringing, it's a number I don't recognize so I ignore the call. The same number calls again, and this time I answer. "This is MyeZelle Washington. How may I assist you?" "Umm, Mrs. Henderson, this is Gabriel, you have a visitor, a Ms. Porter," he questions. "Yes, of course Gabriel, please send her up, thank you!" I'm not sure why but I'm extremely nervous as I walk down the long hall to the living area and await Vic to arrive. I hear the faint sound of the elevator stopping on our floor and I open the door for Vic. Surprisingly, she's smiling! Without a word between us, I usher Victoria in and close the door behind us. She doesn't say a word, Vic is looking around the open space, somewhat amazed.

I relax on the sofa while Vic decides to take a tour without asking or wanting an escort. Victoria returns after prancing down the hall and into the master bedroom. No doubt her nosy ass checked out my closet. She then navigates her way upstairs and checks out all the rooms before returning to the living area. As she sits close to me the interrogation begins. "So slut, I see you and Ron already have the kids' bedrooms set up and you're clearly familiar with the master bed. So, when is the divorce and when is the wedding," laughing hysterically? Victoria can be such a bitch! Ron is right about one thing; she does act as if we're still having threesomes and fucking. "If you are done with your bitch mode, I can let you know what's going on or I can." Before I can read Vic from A-Z my phone rings and its Keenan. "Hey Kee," trying my best to sound excited! "What's up baby, how is everything on the home-front," he questions. I glance over my new home and reply, "everything is great on the home-front, how are you, we miss you," I lie! "So listen Mye, I've decided to take the job with Shapiro and before you cuss me out or hang up, just listen to me okay." I keep my mouth shut, if Keenan only knew how excited I am to be rid of him! "I'm going to make it work Mye, I promise baby. I'll keep our family together and when this is all over, you will appreciate the sacrifice." "I know Kee, but I don't want to move the kids. Minnetonka is all they know. That being said, I know how important this is to you, but I would prefer if we talked about when you get back home at the end of the week, you know, face to face honey." Keenan agrees and we discuss the kids and mundane subjects before ending the call with an I love you. I'm not so sure I meant it but I'm finding myself lying more and more these days and its becoming second nature. Now that Keenan has been taken care of for the day, my attention returns to Victoria.

"As I was saying before I was interrupted, if you're over being bitchy, I can fill you in on what's going on or I can keep it to myself and tell you to mind the business that actually pays you," I bark! Vic understands that I mean business and relaxes. I spill all the tea on what Ron and I have been up to, what Ron really wants and how I really feel. "Vic, I really did try to fight my feelings initially, but the truth is, I like Ron. I've actually fallen hard for him and now I need to figure out how to juggle both." "The good news MyeZelle, your husband won't be home for a few days so you're free to play house with your boytoy a little while longer. What's better, Keenan will be moving soon to Memphis, school will be over so you can ship the kids off for vacation with Daddy for a couple weeks. The only problem I see, Kee already thinks you're doing something wrong and his flunky, Justin is now and will be his eyes and ears." I hear everything she's saying, and Vic is one hundred percent right! With Keenan being away, there's no telling who he will have watching our home, following me and God knows what else!

As Vic and I share a couple cocktails and plenty of laughter, I again hear the faint sound of the elevator, Ron's home. As he enters, I can see Victoria become a bit rattled, it's not anger but fear in her eyes. I squeeze her hand gently and it seems to calm her a bit. "Hey ladies," Ron exclaims with a warm smile." "Hey honey, Vic and I was just catching up," I reply nervously. "Ron listen," Victoria interjects, "I don't want to have a problem with you, I'm just trying to look out for my girl and what's best for her. I apologize if I've overstepped and boundaries with you. I'm very protective of MyeZelle and my God children." Neither Ron nor I can believe what we just heard, was that a stamp of approval?! "Aye Victoria, I get it and I'm sorry for snapping on you. I guess we both are passionate when it comes to this lady right here, it's all good." "Ron, I need to change and get home to check on my babies, get them squared away and get back." "Handle your business baby, I'll be here when you get back home." After bidding Vic a farewell, I quickly change clothes, kiss Ron goodbye and make my way to Minnetonka to check on my babies and ensure they see things as normal with the exception of their father being out of town on business.

✑ Keenan

Man, I thought I would have to check my wife's tongue to get her to listen to me but to my surprise she was receptive to the move. After getting MyeZelle on board, it's time to call Shapiro and let him know I'm all in. "Keenan Washington for Mr. Shapiro please," responding to his assistant. "Keenan, tell me something good brother," he exclaims! "Well, I spoke with my wife and it's a go for me. She's unsure of moving the entire family but I'm definitely taking the offer if and only if I can bring partner along for the ride." "Look brother, you can bring whoever makes you feel comfortable to get this job done. Let's meet tomorrow to go over the paperwork, give you time to send it to your partner, lawyer and anyone else you need to get this contract signed and get the money rolling in." Brad and I discuss a few possibilities for the new subdivision before ending the call. Now, all there is left to do is take care of a few loose ends in Minneapolis, namely Lindsey and this pregnancy.

"Lindsey, you know who this is, call me back," I scream into the phone! So now this bitch is playing games and refuse to answer my calls! "Aryah, how are you baby," I ask softly. "Mando, I miss you, how are," she responds gleefully! "I'm good baby girl, I miss you too! What are you up to?" Aryah explains she's home, bored out of her freaking mind! "Listen, can you get away for a few days?" "Of course I can, Randall is still in the doghouse. I can go and do whatever I want right now, what's up?" "Check on flights leaving Minneapolis tonight coming to Memphis. I want to spend the rest of my week here with you and celebrate." "Are you serious Mando, I would absolutely love that!" "Find a ticket, pack light and call me back. Tell your husband you need to be with one of your sorority sisters or something, anything to get you on that plane." "Don't worry Mando, if I can get a ticket tonight, I will see you tonight. Trust me, if he wasn't in the doghouse, he still wouldn't care! Honestly Mando, I think he and Lindsey are still screwing around. I wouldn't be surprised if the baby turns out to be his but enough about that. I'll check the flights and call you back shortly!"

Listening to Aryah has totally pissed me off again! I still can't believe this hoe cheated on me! Does she know I can destroy her?! "So you're answering your phone now white trash," I scream into the phone! "Keenan I'm in the hospital! I couldn't answer my phone when you called!" After a long pause, I finally respond, "so what's going on," I ask curious. "If you really want to know, I started cramping and bleeding vaginally. The doctors gave me an exam and an ultrasound. I'm 9 weeks pregnant Keenan and the baby is healthy." "Linds, I'm sorry I went crazy, but we have to take care of this baby. I need you all to myself and a baby is going to mess all that up! Don't you get that," I plead! "No Keenan, what I get is you're the most selfish man I've ever met. I'm sure Aryah will keep you occupied just to spite me! I'm keeping our baby and you will continue to take care of me if you want to keep your little family together!" Furious, I rant, "if you think for one minute that you can threaten me with your bastard baby, you have another thing coming! Lindsey, I can ruin you, and I can make sure that baby is never born! You're a drug and alcohol addicted whore who nobody wants including," the phone goes dead. This whore hung up on me! I try calling back but her phone is going straight to voicemail. I try sending a text but that doesn't go through either, she's blocked me!

I reach for the Henny and take a few shots. I can't believe the balls on this bitch. She's now bold enough to threaten me and my family. Shit is getting wild! Just when I thought enough to use the hotel phone to reach her, Aryah calls. "Mando, there's a flight tonight on Delta Airlines leaving the Twin Cities at 8:44 and arriving in Memphis at 10:48, is that okay," she asks in an almost child-like voice. "That's perfect baby girl. You don't have that much time so throw a couple things in a bag, text me your address and I'll have a car pick you up at exactly 7. Your ticket will be waiting for you." "I will be ready Mando, will you be picking me up or will it be someone else?" "You'll receive a text letting you know what to do, don't worry baby, I'm going to take care of you, I promise." After hanging up with Aryah, I realize I haven't talked to Justin at all today and give him a buzz. "Big Kee, what's going on brother?" "Hey man, I got some great news! MyeZelle is on board with the project in Memphis so we're a go! Speaking of MyeZelle, do you have any information for me?" "Actually yeah, I do." Justin pauses and I feel a sudden sharp pain in the center of my chest. "Kee, MyeZelle not on nothing man! Other than getting too litty with Vic's crazy ass, your wife is doing absolutely nothing. I told you man, she's mean and crazy but she also loyal. You don't have nothing to worry about brother!" Damn, Justin could have said that straight out! "Man, you almost made my heart stop pausing like that, shit!" "Yeah, if you feel like that, maybe you should focus on your wife and leave these knuckle head hoes alone, you in enough shit already with Lindsey and now the Armenian broad? Come on man, give ya dick a rest brother, enough is enough!" Justin's absolutely right. I've gotten myself into some real life bullshit this time with Lindsey and this baby but I'm too far in to turn back now. Besides, I've already promised Aryah she's gonna be number one for the next few days. "I know brother, good thing Mye is on board with this job so I can get the hell out town, far away from crazy Lindsey," I laugh! "I get it brother, so when do we move cause I'm in the same boat! I came home this morning to Carrina screaming and walking out of the door saying she wants a divorce!" "Damn J, I'm sorry to hear that," I respond. "Brother don't be sorry for me! I've been trying to get rid of this farm girl turned Larsa Pippen wannabe bitch! She waits til she's forty to wanna turn up and party and be seen, I'm good brother! Just let me know when to start packing my shit so I can get the hell out of town too," he laughs. After we share more "crazy ass women" stories I end the call and hit the shower.

I use Shapiro's driver to scoop Aryah from the airport. After showing the guy a photo of Aryah, he was more than happy to greet her at baggage claim. After waiting for half an hour, they finally make it to the car. Aryah is a stunningly beautiful woman! Tonight, she has a different glow about her. As she slides in the backseat next to me, without saying a word, I grab her head to pull her close to me and stick my tongue down her throat. We kiss passionately for a minute before I need to catch my breath. Aryah's rocking a Balenciaga short, grey mini dress. A man shouldn't know that type of shit but the name is splattered all over the dress so there you have it! "You look beautiful sweetheart." "Thank you Mando, that was quite a kiss," she snickers. "Yeah, I know baby," I respond as i pull her closer.

On the way back to the hotel, Aryah rests her head on my chest and falls asleep. I unzip my pants and push her head down. You don't get any naps on my dime unless I'm already sleep! Initially, she had no idea what was going on and looked up at me in bewilderment. "He needs a kiss too baby." Without needing to say another word, Aryah wraps her lips around my hard dick and go to work. Shapiro's driver must be used to shit like this cause soon as Aryah's mouth wrapped around the tip of my dick, a blackout partition emerges from the floor and we're in complete darkness.

Aryah has A1 head game. She deep throats my entire shaft going up and down slowly while massaging my nuts with one hand. "Damn you on that dick baby. Ooooooh shit, play with that head baby, yeah, suck that head for me!" I push her head back all the way down and fuck her face until I bust in her mouth. The girl didn't choke, gag, nothing! Once I made her swallow my kids, I allowed her to sit back up in time to arrive back at the hotel. After tipping Shapiro's driver, I let him know I will need him in a couple of hours after I allow Aryah to freshen up.

I order Aryah to take a shower while I fix myself a drink and relax on the sofa. Downtown is bustling on a Wednesday night and Beale Street is crowded from my vantage point. I must have been in my own world because I didn't see or hear Aryah approaching me naked and still dripping wet. "Mando, Mando, are you here with me or somewhere else," she asks. "No, I'm here with you, just got a lot on my mind. Some of it I need to talk to you about, but we'll get into that later. Right now, I need you to get on the bed, spread your legs and that pussy wide open for me baby!" "Play with your pussy for me baby," I command as I remove my clothing. I watch Aryah as she plays with her fat pussy, moaning softly as she begs me touch her. "Mando please, I need you so badly," pleading with me! Finally, I pull her to the edge of the bed, legs in the air and command her to spread them pussy lips open for me and keep them open. Once she complies, my lips cover her clit and I swirl my tongue around. Less than a minute goes by before Aryah begins shaking uncontrollably! I flip her on her stomach and slowly push my dick deep inside her tight walls. As I stroke her, the urge to nut becomes strong so I pull out and force my dick in her ass. Aryah lets out a scream and before I can pull out, my nut goes off inside her ass. I fall on Aryah's back and have to lay there for a minute.

After Aryah and I shower together, we dress and hit Beale Street for a late dinner and some blues from B.B. King's place. As we walk in, hand-in-hand, all male's eyes in the place are fixated on Aryah and their old, jealous, fat ass wives have looks that could kill. There are a couple of interracial couples also enjoying the music and drinks, but they don't hold a candle to us! I can be King of Bluff City with this woman on my arm!

ᴄ&ᴏ Lindsey

I'm so emotionally and physically drained. The stress of dealing with Keenan's anger and resentment has taken a toll. Adding Aryah to the mix to humiliate me just exacerbated the drama. I'm fully aware that I really screwed up my friendship with Aryah by sleeping with Randall but when you forgive someone you're supposed to move forward and clearly, she has replaced forgiveness with vengeance. I really need Aryah and I'm desperate, I have no else I can confide in! I phone her and it rings several times before she finally picks up. "Hello", she answers dryly. "Hi Aryah, it's Lindsey". "Yes, I know what's up I'm a little busy". I was wondering if you could come to Abbott Northwestern, I came close to suffering a miscarriage and I really need someone", I plead. "I'm sorry Lindsey, I'm out of town sweetie. I'm in Myrtle Beach visiting a sorority sister. I'm sorry you're in the hospital. I'll call when I get back to Minneapolis, ok dear?" Saddened and crying at her response I agree and end the call. I'm not sure if I'm more saddened by the fact that Aryah just blatantly lied to me or that I really hoped we could past everything. It's not as if she's innocent in this situation. Aryah begged me to have a threesome with her husband, what did she think was going to happen! There were several occasions where she directed Randall and I on what to do while she recorded. Did she really think he would only want me when she was around?

"Hey Randall, are you busy, I need to talk to someone." I know I shouldn't call him but I have no one else to turn to that would come close to understanding the situation I find my in. "Yeah, how you doing Lindsey, I got time. Aryah went to Miami to visit a girlfriend from college, what's up?" Visiting a girlfriend in Florida my ass "When did she leave, do you know who she went to visit", I ask. "Nah man, all I know is her flight left at 8:45 and she called me when she landed a couple hours later. She gone for a few days so I don't have to deal with her damn mouth. Whatchu on?" I know where this is going and even if I wanted to, I can't. "I'm in the hospital, I'm 9 weeks pregnant and almost suffered a miscarriage", I respond very bluntly. "Damn shorty, I hate to hear that, what hospital you at, I'll slide on you after I take care of some business." I give Randall my info and her reassures me that I'll see him tonight. Aws horrible as I felt for cheating with Randall behind Aryah's back, he and I developed a close friendship in the process. He's a guy from the hood but he also has a big heart and he's showing it.

I called Keenen several times and was repeatedly sent to voicemail. Keenan is in Memphis on business and I suspect that bitch Aryah is with him! Flights from Minneapolis to Memphis are at least three hours minimum and Randall stated Aryah called within a couple hours of departing Minneapolis, no way she made it that fast! I hop online to find out what flights departed tonight from Minneapolis-Saint Paul and bingo! The lone flight leaving between 8:30 and 9:00 was bound for Memphis Tennessee! I send Keenan and Aryah a group text. "I know where you two scum-of-the-earth fucks are! Keenan, I have you by the balls and YOU WILL take care of our child or your precious little BLACK QUEEN will find out she has an addition to her perfect little family! As for you Aryah, Randall should have left you where he found you. You're a fucking looser CUNT! And did you tell your new boyfriend that the only reason I started sleeping with your husband is because you asked me to?! First the threesomes then he and I one-on-one while you recorded the entire thing! That's right Keenan, you're with a scandalous manipulator who used you to hurt me after she asked me to fuck her husband! I'm going to destroy both of you the way you have tried to destroy me"! I can see Keenan wrapping his hands around Aryah's throat right now and my stress and sadness has been replaced with a huge smile and satisfaction!

Unsure of how long I've been asleep, I awake to Randall stroking my hair. "Oh my God, Randall! How long have you been here", I ask in a whisper. "A couple hours but I didn't want to wake you, you were snoring shorty so you needed that sleep", he laughs and continues. "I don't know how your phone didn't wake you up, that nigga that got you knocked up been blowing ya damn phone all the way up! Aryah called a couple times too so I finally turned ya shit off man." "Thank you for coming it means a lot." "So whatchu gone do shorty, you gone keep that nigga baby knowing he ain't never gone leave his wife and kids?" I sigh, "I've already had one abortion, I just can't go through another one. I can take care of my baby on my own." "Look shorty, if you gone keep yo baby, make that nigga pay! His money long, you shoulda been making that sucka muthafuka pay every time he hit the pussy, fuck cause he pay yo bills, he posed to do that shit too!" Randall continues to vent his frustration for the next half hour and I keep quiet and listen. His approach and style of speaking may be harsh but he's absolutely right. All I ever wanted from Keenan was love and attention and, in the beginning, he showered me with both. It seems as if he changed overnight! He suddenly became very critical of everything I did: the way I cooked, clean, dressed, wore my hair, everything. His sexual appetite became increasing rough as well. It went from a light spanking on my derriere bruises left behind, holding my neck to choking, different men, different women. He's forced me to accompany him to swingers' parties. Everything Keenan has done, I chalked it up to him having an insatiable sexual appetite. I now realize it wasn't so much he needed these things; it was to humiliate me to the point I would feel completely worthless and forced to totally depend on him. I now must figure out on my own how to keep me and my baby safe. "Randall, do you think you stay with me tonight since Aryah's in Miami?" He stares into my eyes, "yeah shorty, I gotchu. I know you ain't really got nobody and I know dat nigga don't want another baby so ima stay up here in case he wanna try some stupid shit. You know I ain't fa none!" I fain sadness, "he's actually in Memphis on a business trip for the next three or four days. This big wig out of LA wants him to head up a project in Memphis. He tried wooing him by sending a private jet which is ridiculous! I mean Memphis is only a two or three hour flight from us, you know", shrugging my shoulders.

Randall remains quiet and I'm hoping the wheels are starting to spin in his head but I continue just in case he hasn't gotten the hint. "He's such an asshole, I hope he stays in Memphis so that I can enjoy my pregnancy and deliver a healthy baby, even if I do have to go through this alone. Maybe Aryah will truly forgive me eventually you know." Randall just listens so I continue, "The last time she came to visit, we made up and when Keenan showed up unannounced, everything changed. They both left angry with me. Aryah was full of hate and Keenan wanted to kill me even after I told him I was pregnant with his child! They both stormed out and left me just standing there like the biggest loser but that doesn't matter now. I just want to keep my baby safe." Randall stands and walks over to the window to stare out at the street and cars below.

"So my wife met that nigga", he questions. "Yes, I'm sorry, I didn't mean to upset you. I thought she would have you; I mean with news of my pregnancy and all." We both fall silent and I drift into a deep sleep.

Morning came and Randall was still there, staring out the window. I clear my throat to get his attention. He turns, "morning' shorty, feeling better?" "Good morning, yeah actually, I feel much better, thank you for staying, it meant so much to me." "Man shorty, we always gone be good, you already know. Look man, I gotta ride but I'll slide on you later, if they let you out, hit me up." Without waiting on a response, Randall bolted for the door.

Once I'm sure he's gone, I decide to give Mr. Washington a call. He's blown my phone up all night right along with Aryah. I'm hoping Randall was awake to witness the panic and desperation from both. If he hasn't caught on by now, he will. "What do you want Keenan", I scream into the phone upon hearing his "Lindsey, what?" "Lindsey what in the hell is going on with you? Has this pregnancy already drove you crazy or is it all the drugs?" "Keenan cut the crap! I know Aryah is there with you. For your sake, you better pray her husband doesn't find out because you're not capable of handling a man like that! He would totally beat you out of those three piece designer suits you're so proud to wear!" The silence is deafening! "Lindsey, I don't take kindly to threats, there's a better way we can work this out without destroying people's lives, don't you think baby?" Did this asshole really just call me baby?! "Going forward, you will address me as Lindsey or Ms. Mahommes, I'm not your fucking baby! We will work out what I want worked out! You will continue to pay all my bills, including all medical expenses and anything else I fucking want! When you return from your little trick vacation, I want to see a deposit of no less than one million to start. I want monthly payments of fifteen thousand and those numbers are not negotiable! One other thing, don't ever show up to my condo again unannounced! And just in case you're thinking of doing something crazy, I retained an attorney who knows everything and how to proceed should I have some sort of accident or break a fucking fingernail! You and that cunt Aryah deserve one another, your both trash!" I end the call before giving Keenan an opportunity to respond.

After spending a few days in the hospital, my doctors release me with strict instructions going forward: no stress, no alcohol, no drugs! The alcohol and drugs aren't my issue, trying to remain stress free could be a challenge. Keenan has no conscience when it comes to him and what he wants and that's frightening. I'm praying he's going accept my demands and walk away but my gut instinct tells me he's going to do everything within his power to destroy me! He doesn't have a compromising bone in his body, least not when it comes to me!

✑ MyeZelle

On my way to pick Kee up from the airport, thoughts of Ron consume me. This past week has been incredible! We were an actual couple for a short time and I felt my soul return, I was alive again and not just going through the motions of my life! Ronald has rejuvenated me and I don't want to go back. I'm not going back! I've come up with the perfect plan! This week was the last week of school for my babies and what better way to kick of the summer than hanging with their dad in Memphis. It's already hot there compared to Minnesota. Keenan would have to focus on the kids versus whore chasing and I'll be free to find out how real this thing between Ron and I really is!

"Welcome home honey," mustering up as much enthusiasm as possible. "What's going on baby, how's the crew?" "They're great, ready for their favorite dad to come home!" "That's not saying much, I'm the only dad," he responds with a chuckle. We spend the drive home discussing the new deal with Shapiro and the huge impact this project could have on our family. After pulling into garage, I give Keenan a very passionate kiss and assure him I'm in favor of the move. "We just have to come up with a plan that's best for us both and the kids." "I know baby, let's just relax tonight, we have all weekend to get a plan together," he replies.

As we enter the kitchen, we're immediately greeted by all four children with a poster board reading, "WELCOME HOME DAD, WHEN IS VACATION!". We all burst into synchronized laughter. After chatting with our children, I order them to bed. School may be out but it's close to midnight though I doubt they'll go to sleep.

Keenan and I retire to our bedroom to relax while watching a movie. Before the previews are over, he begins placing his fingers inside me. There's no way in hell I'm having sex with Keenan tonight, husband or not! To throw him off, I switch it up, "I miss you too baby, let me show you how much!" Though it turned my stomach thinking about wrapping my lips around his dick, I knew I had to! There was no feeling of love or any emotion as I sucked him to the point where he was ready. When the time came, I snatched his dirty dick out of my mouth and let his cum shoot any and everywhere but in or on me! There is no way in hell Keenan will ever have the privilege of my "swallowing" again! Although he seemed puzzled, I convinced him I watched a porno while he was away, saw the exact same thing and wanted to see how high his cum would shoot up! We both laughed and he fell asleep before I could decide on another movie!

On Saturday, we decided to go out on Lake Minnetonka for a family outing. "Kee, I'm going to call Vic and invite her if she doesn't have any plans so why don't you ask Justin to come along as well but minus his wife?" "Alright baby," he laughs, "we can do that. It is a beautiful day out and I don't think we have to worry anymore about her, Justin's getting rid of her once and for all!" Once we confirm Justin and Victoria will join us, we load up the troops and make our way to the lake.

"Hey girl, how did you beat us here," addressing Victoria as I exit the family SUV. "I was already in the area having a drink with a potential client Pooh. What's going on with you, you're glowing", she smirks. "You're such a twot! I would call you something else but your god children as present," I respond along with a pinch to her arm. I'm certain Vic will have my front, back and sides forever but she enjoys reveling in bullshit and stirring the pot. "Girls, girls, girls, can we board and get everyone comfortable before all the catfighting," Keenan interjects. The sound of his voice is making my skin crawl. I hurry the children aboard and they make a mad dash for the lounge area. Once I've settled the trips down and get them squared away, Victoria and I make our way to the top deck and strip down to our bikinis to enjoy the Jacuzzi. Keenan and Justin join us a short time later with drinks in hand. "Honey, Vic and I would like some drinks as well." "Damn baby, you and Vic are as bad as the kids! You two wasted no time getting your relaxation on I see." As I give him "the look", he continues, "alright baby, I'll grab you Queens some drinks, is there anything else I can do for Your Majesties," he jokes. I clap back, "yes peasant, there is! Make sure everything is stocked we'll need before we anchor up. Oh and one more thing honey, bring up towels and a fruit platter." Keenan grunts as he and Justin retreat downstairs.

After relaxing in the Jacuzzi for over an hour, Vic and I dry off and join Keenan and Justin in the upper deck lounge area. We all remain silent for a while and just take in the view. The lake is plentiful with couples and families enjoying a rare hot day for this time of year. Minnesota normally doesn't get really hot until July. I focus my attention on an older couple nearby on a sailboat. They're wrapped in each other's arms as a new couple would. They're smiling and looking into each other's eyes and I find myself being envious. I'm positive they've been together for decades judging by their age, but the love is still new. I want that so badly and as I turn to see Keenan laughing and joking with Justin, I know deep in my heart I can never have that long standing love with him as I thought I would.

I don't want it with him anymore! My thoughts are of Ron, where things are and where they go from here.

"So Justin, how's your wife," I ask breaking the silence and knowing the answer. "Well," he begins, "she should be better now that she's soon to be back in Amish country," he laughs monstrously. I'm puzzled, what is he talking about! "What do you mean," curiously I ask. "Umm MyeZelle, lay off the Ciroc hun, damn you didn't catch that," Vic blurts out. After a couple seconds, I do get it. "Yeah Mye, she wants a divorce, and I couldn't be happier! You saw how she changed up on me as soon as we got married! In the beginning, I was all in until her ass went all "Hollywood" on me. I don't want or need that in my life, what I need is a ride or die like you. I need Vic!" Justin immediately turned to Victoria, and she was ready, as always! "Boy bye," Vic laughs hysterically! "You couldn't handle me when I was willing to give you a shot! You definitely can't handle me now! You have too many bitches and I would hate to drag one of them, your wife included! Hell, I'll drag her ass for you without getting involved with you, that right there my friend will cost you nothing at all!" We all burst into laughter.

I interrupt the fun and ask Vic to accompany me downstairs to check on the children. Once we're out of earshot, I turn to Vic, "can you believe she's leaving him," I ask in amazement! "Hell yeah, I can believe it and Justin is right! He was actually being a good man when he thought he married a wholesome Amish chic. That bitch couldn't wait to do a one hundred eighty degree turn once she got a taste of the world!" Vic continues, "remember we welcomed her and everything was cool. When we took her under our wing and showed her ways to style her hair, beat her face and dress, Carrina went brand new right along with her new fashion sense. I don't really care if he leaves or she leaves as long as we don't have deal with her ass anymore!"

Vic reminds me so much of "Tasha" from "Why Did I get Married! "Girl let's get dinner out for the kids, you are so right but so damn crazy." I laugh as we continue to the kitchen. I don't bother interrupting the kids as I can hear the girls laughing in their room and the twins are doing their usual in the lounge area at the center of boat, playing Fortnite. After preparing the troops' dinner and rounding them up to eat, Vic and I return upstairs to join Keenan and Justin who by now are at the very least tipsy!

"So, I guess we're staying out on the lake tonight." I mean, we can, I just can't get too full and lay my phone anywhere! "I can get Vic and J back to the dock if they have something going on. I mean, Vic may but my man here doesn't have home obligations it seems anymore! Man J, I want to be like you when I grow up!" "Be careful what you wish for honey, you just may get it," I snap back.

As the night progresses, the four of us laugh and joke of old times and everything seems normal. I know it's not. My body is here but my mind is far away. I don't have the discipline it seems to separate my family life and this new life from Ron anymore. I excuse myself and make my way to the primary quarters and phone Ron. His cell rings several times before he finally answers. "What's up sweetheart, I've been thinking about you all day!" After my heart settles back down, I eventually respond, "hey honey, I've been thinking about you as well, that's why I'm calling," I laugh. I give him an update on what I've been doing and he's not too happy I'm spending time with my husband so I try appeasing him. "Honey look, I have to play the role right now for my kids, but I do have some news I think will put your mind at ease. Just let me do what I need to do and everything will be okay I promise." "I know you got to do what you got to do, I just miss your fine ass and want to be with you every day. I need to see you tomorrow if just for a little while." I agree and end the call. I need to get back above deck before anyone misses me.

Upon returning to the group, I notice Keenan is off to the side on his phone and Justin and Victoria are at it again! I promise, whenever these two have a drink, they go back and forth as if they're the married couple in the group! "Hey," I yell, "do you two need a room or what!" We all burst into laughter and of course, Vic is the first to plead her case. "Mye, now you know how this man is! Every time we get together, he starts talking shit about how I should have been his wife, blah, blah, blah! Once again, I had to tell him, he can't handle me Pooh. He knows this! I'm too much woman for him and I would have to whip Justin's ass for playing with me!" Justin can't control his laughter as Vic continues. "Do you see the type of woman he married?" Turning her attention to Justin, she continues, "that thing you married and me are day and night! I will have your ass running around in the daytime with a flashlight looking for me!" Tears are now rolling down my face from laughter. My girl is so wild and so damn entertaining! We spend the rest of the night drinking, joking, laughing and before long, the sun was rising on us.

After a hot shower, I dress and check on the kids but they're all sleeping. Once I get them moving, Vic and I start breakfast for everyone. I tackle the sausage, bacon, waffles and eggs while I let Vic get the fruit together, I don't think the girl can broil an egg without burning it! Once we're all seated, Vic offers the prayer over breakfast, and it started as a very simple, normal prayer over a meal until she got towards the end. "Jesus, I also ask you to guide Keenan as he takes my godchildren on this summer vacation to Memphis. Lord, guide him so that he understands that he will have to be both husband and wife. That he will have to be chef and maid with the help of my godchildren. We ask all these things in your name Jesus, let us all say Amen," she concludes.

What in the name of all fuckery was that?! Keenan is glaring at me as he is as perplexed as I. Justin is just trying to keep himself from falling over in his seat from having too much to drink along with Vic's prayer! Victoria has her head still bowed with a smirk on her face and the kids have all jumped from the table screaming and dancing in excitement! I was on the phone with Ron less than, five minutes, what could I have possibly missed! Keenan interrupts the silent tension, "Vic, what the hell are you talking about," he demands in an almost whisper as not to alert the children. "What do you mean, what am I talking about Keenan. I told you last night about this upcoming murder trial Mye and I have undertaken and how high-profiled it's going to be and the time we're going to need to focus and prepare! You, "Mr. Almighty" volunteered, "well my kids coming with me for the summer anyway so they can learn some new shit!" That's what you said. You also said your wife can do the traveling back and forth and you and Rosie got this! Do you not remember that conversation Kee?" Vic glares back at Keenan while Justin and I are both in a state of shock. "No, Victoria, I don't remember that shit but thank you for making it known to everyone at the breakfast table! Clearly I had too much to drink but now I have to go along with your drunk shenanigans and setup, at least for a couple weeks. Look at the way my kids are running around!" Keenan points to the twins still high fiving, while our girls are still shrieking and dancing. I know my girl is crazy, but she talked my husband into this? This right here is some wickedly clever shit and I love it!

We all managed to get through breakfast without alerting the kids to any discourse. Keenan instructs our Captain to head back to the docks as he and Justin disappear back on top deck. Vic and I return to the kitchen to clean and I finally get the chance to bring up "the breakfast prayer". "Girl, what was that? Did Kee really say all that?" My back-to-back questions seemed to frustrate Vic. "Yes, damn it, he said ALL THAT! You know how your husband is "Big Willie" once he's lit, he can do no wrong, can do it all, has everything under control all at the same damn time! All I did was give his ass enough rope to hang himself," she laughs and continues. You can thank me later missy. You now have time to really find out what Ron is about. He's either a Godsend or the devil in disguise but I digress and you're welcome!" "What murder case are you talking about Vic, please tell me not the quadruple homicide that's made national news." "Look, while I was downtown, I met with the guy. He doesn't have a lawyer yet and while I didn't say that we would take the case, I did tell him we would both meet with him next week and discuss it. Girl, I just got you a "hot girl" summer, free of kids! All you have to do is make sure Bonnie and Clyde are good and Natalie can do that since Rosie is going with Keenan and the kids. Besides, if we choose not to take the case, Keenan doesn't have to know that shit until after he and the kids are already gone! Now can we go back up before he and Justin cook up some bullshit and ruin this plan?" I agree to table our discussion until we return to the office on Monday.

We finally arrive home after saying our goodbyes to Victoria and Justin. The kids make their way to the family room still in party mode and Keenan ushers me to our bedroom to discuss the "breakfast prayer" revelation. He doesn't wastes anytime going in either. "What the hell is wrong with Vic bringing that bullshit up at the table this morning in front of our kids," he bemoans. "Kee, I don't understand what the issue is. You chose to jump in that water with no life jacket and I can't save you so I suggest you get your ass back to Memphis and get a home set up for our children for the summer!" I continue before Keenan has a chance to respond. "You cannot and will not disappoint them! They're over the moon right now on the idea that they get to live in a totally new state for the summer so I suggest you figure it out and fast!" "Yeah, I'll figure it out but that tricky ass best friend of yours did that shit on purpose. So, I guess the two of you have plans hoe around while I'm hundreds of miles away taking care of our kids huh MyeZelle," he barks! I would tell him to kiss my ass but he would enjoy that too much! "Keenan, you whore around for the both of us and darling if I wanted to cheat on you, I can do it right under your nose. You wouldn't have to be in another state. Fortunately for you, I have a moral compass and not enough time for another headache of a man!" Yes, I lied and with a straight face! I learned that shit from him!

✑ Keenan

That damn Victoria is an evil witch and my wife is right there with her! This was some sort of plot to stick me with our children so she can try to keep me on lockdown while I'm out of town! MyeZelle should know I'm always a couple steps ahead! We eventually call a truce and fall asleep after going round and around.

I'm in the office by 7am the next day with a plan. The first thing I do is text Lindsey. After a couple hours go by with no response, I try calling several times without success. A short time after lunch, Lindsey finally returns my calls. "Baby girl, I've been waiting all day for you to get back with me. Listen can you come to my office, I want to talk to you about us and the baby." There's a long pause before Lindsey finally responds. "I don't trust you Keenan so I think I'll pass." "Damn it Lindsey, I'm trying to work this out with you. What could I possibly do at my office? My building is surrounded by cameras both inside and out. I have a way for us to work this thing out and eventually be together. I just need to go over things with you in person, I would never hurt you or our baby," I plead. "I'll be there in about an hour Keenan!"

Lindsey finally arrives after making me wait for over two hours. This bitch is going to milk this pregnancy thing for all its worth! "I see you finally made it!" I greet her, trying not to sound too irritated. "You're lucky I showed at all and I don't really have any more of my life or time to waste on you Keenan so what is this about?" "Damn baby girl you don't love me no more," I question as I close the door to my office. "Sit down Lindsey, you just might like what I'm about to propose, sit down baby." Lindsey studies me up and down before finally feeling comfortable enough to take a seat. "Lindsey, you don't have to be afraid of me. I'm not going to hurt you or our baby. I guess I was just in shock that you were pregnant again and I didn't take it well." "Didn't take it well? Keenan, you humiliated me in front of that bitch Aryah and you threatened me! That's a bit more than just not taking it well, don't you think," she screams! "Look, I was wrong and I'm sorry. I'll be moving to Memphis next week for a least a year, possibly two. I wanted to know if you would come with me. My wife and I are separating and she's agreed to let me have my kids for the summer. We can be a family like you wanted, that is what you still want right?" "I don't know what to say Keenan, why the sudden about face?" "You know I love you. When I found out you cheated on me, I was angry, but I understand why. You were lonely and I was going home to my family not taking your feelings into consideration. I'm sorry and I want to make it up to you, if you'll allow me to." Several minutes passed before Lindsey finally responded to my offer. "How do I know that you're not going to go back to your wife and what about that bitch Aryah?! Exactly what do you plan to do about her," she counters! "I broke it off with Aryah once I came back. I only fucked with her to get back at you. It's over Lindsey, I just want you, my baby and my kids. We can start over, like a real family this time!" "I don't know Kee, you want me to just pick up my entire life and move away with you. How do I know I can trust you after everything that's happened?" We go back and forth until I finally convince her. "I have a suite at the Westin. All you need to do is get your clothes together over the next few days. We'll fly out together and find a house. Whatever house you want baby, I promise." I walk over to Lindsey and pull her into my arms and hold her for a while. "I'm gonna make sure you get everything you deserve baby, just trust me," I whisper into Lindsey's ear. After a long cry, she finally gets herself together and I reiterate the importance of getting to Memphis as quickly as possible. Lindsey promises to pack a few bags and await my instructions.

"Justin, can I see you in my office, I need to go over some things with you." I must tell J exactly what my intentions are! He'll let me know if I've completely lost my mind! "No problem, let me wrap up this e-mail and I'll be right there," Justin responds. After keeping me waiting for close to a half hour, J finally enters my office and I waste no time giving him all the details of my diabolical plan. By the end, Justin's jaw has dropped and his eyes are bulging out of his head as if he's seen a ghost! "Kee, have you lost all touch with reality? You seriously have to be out of your fucking mind to think you can actually get away with something like this!" "Shit isn't as complicated as people make it out to be man! It could work," I plead. "Kee, you're going to lose a hell of a lot more than your family if you choose to go ahead with this crazy ass plan. I don't understand how you would consider something so fucked up! I'm always gonna have your back but I be damned if I lose my freedom cause you on some bullshit brother, you're taking this too far man! I suggest you pay this bitch off and force her into another abortion or get ready to face the consequences with your wife which just might be worse than losing everything you've worked for, hell we've worked for, together!" "What else can I do? This bitch is extorting me at this point! I told you what she wants, I retort!" "Yeah, you told me, and

I suggest giving Lindsey whatever she wants if it's going to keep her mouth shut, you out of prison and MyeZelle from completely destroying you," Justin counters. I know he's right, but I can't take a chance on this broad double crossing me! The minute she finds out I'm still seeing Aryah, she'll sing like that lil rap nigga 6ix9ine to my wife and anyone else who's willing to listen! I change subjects as I'm getting nowhere with Justin on this fiasco I've created for myself!

"So J, when are you going to make the move to Memphis?" "I don't know man seeing as though I'm going to be getting a divorce, I don't really see a point in getting a house. Shapiro said he'd foot any hotel costs. I figure, I'll get a suite and make that work. I don't have a reason to rent or purchase anything big." I think for a moment and come up with a plan B to go along with plan A. "So why don't we do like we did here. Same deal as our condo, only this would be a side-by-side duplex. And, you would only have to kick in one third and we'll have a crib, you know with a yard pool, hot tub. We're gonna need amenities like that in Memphis brother, trust me. The heat is already on hell there," I embellish somewhat. "As long as you've come to your senses about this Lindsey thing, you know I'm with you one hundred percent brother. Just think of the bullshit we can get into once the kids are back here with MyeZelle! Not to mention summers lasts longer in the south so you know them thick ass southern girls are still gonna be walking around half naked in September, probably October too. Not to mention you know most of them can cook like grandma used to," Justin exclaims! "I agree with you brother about the whole Lindsey situation. I'll figure out another way. Look man, I gotta get out of here but I'll give you a call later." I grab my briefcase and phone and rush pass Justin, leaving him sitting alone and somewhat stunned in my office.

"Lindsey baby, pick up." I plead but her phone ultimately goes to voicemail. A few minutes go by before she returns my call. "Damn baby, I started to panic a bit when you didn't answer or call back right away," I lie, AGAIN! "I'm sorry Kee, the morning sickness doesn't just happen in the morning, it's whenever this little person doesn't like what I eat or drink or smell," she laughs. "I'm on my way, I'll bring some soup and crackers baby. Also, I'll grab some ginger ale. Hopefully that'll help settle my soon-to-be mini-me down." "And just what makes you think it's a boy Keenan," she responds. "It doesn't matter if it's a boy or girl, it's still going to be my mini-me. I can feel it! I'll see you soon baby, I love you Lindsey." I hang up before she has a chance to respond.

Once I park, I check my briefcase to make sure I have everything I need. I take a couple shots of Hennessy, blow some "white girl" before making my way upstairs. Lindsey is walking out of the bedroom looking worse for wear as I enter. I smile as I walk past making my way to kitchen to prepare her meal. "Baby relax, let me take care of you. I gotta get you right before you get on that plane in the next few days." "I'm not sure I can keep anything on my stomach Kee." "Didn't I tell you I was gonna take care of you? I stopped by CVS and the pharmacist recommended this nasal spray. The lady said it works better than the pill form because you risk throwing that back up. Here baby, two pumps in each nostril while I warm your soup." Lindsey hesitates briefly. After I reassure her the spray is guaranteed to work, she follows my instructions. I bring her soup and ginger ale and place it on the coffee table in front of her. A short time passes before Lindsey panics! "Keenan," Lindsey screams, "Keenan, something is wrong! Help me, my heart hurts, its beating too fast!" I stand over Lindsey with a glare I'm sure the devil would appreciate! "Please Keenan, what have you done?!" As Lindsey struggles to breath, the savage in me comes out. As I stand over her, I begin to relish in her suffering. "Did you really think I was going to leave my family for you bitch? Do you really think you ever had a fucking chance of replacing my wife," I continue to rant! "If I was going to leave my wife, I wouldn't do it for a hoe ass bitch like you! Now, your ex best friend Aryah, yeah, I might think about it. As a matter of fact, she's going to be spending a lot of time with me and my children in Memphis while you and your fucking baby are pushing up daises! Try to relax, the more you struggle, the quicker you're going to OD!"

I leave Lindsey struggling on the sofa while I proceed to the bedroom to locate the candy dish but it's nowhere to be found. "Where is the candy bowl bitch, I know you didn't get rid of all that dope and pills," I demand! Lindsey can only manage a couple of "helps" before falling unconscious. I remove all my fingerprints from everything I think I've touched and set the scene. After dabbing a minute trace of powder under Lindsey's nose, I scatter the remaining drugs I brought along on the floor and table near her body.

Gathering all my belongings, I calmly walk out into the evening air and make a b-line to my vehicle. I chain smoke Newports while downing more Hennessy before finally heading home. I know I shouldn't pray that everything works out for me but I'm definitely hoping it does. A brother like me isn't built for twenty-five to life! All she had to do was be a side chic but no! As soon as you spoil these side hoes, they get too greedy and too needy! Now, she gets nothing!

✑ MyeZelle

I'm feeling like a teenage girl all over again! Keenan and his "spy" Justin are in Memphis and after two weeks, he's finally settled on a home our children will be comfortable in for the summer! Victoria decided to join me and the troops to Memphis for a few days while I get them settled in. I'm looking forward to spending as much time as possible with Ronald.

I sent Rosie on down last week so she can ensure everything is in order before our arrival. I'm going to certainly miss my children, but I welcome the change! I've been sneaking out of the house each night after eleven and returning at four or five o'clock in the morning just to lay next to Ron for those precious few hours. It gets harder each day to leave him and I have no idea what I'm going to do by summer's end, but I intend to have a "hot girl's summer"!

After dinner, the kids and I are lounging in the family room when the doorbell rings. I'm not expecting anyone so I'm sure it's the case of a lost dog or a kid seeking a few dollars for yard work take care of it. "Mrs. M, there's a Mr. Henderson here to see you, he says it's very important!" What the hell is going on?! Why would Ron pop up at my house when we clearly have a routine established that's been working just fine! "I'll be right there Rosie! Kids, I'll be right back, keep the party going for me okay?" I sprint upstairs, dismiss Natalie's nosy ass and close the front door behind me.

"Ron, what are you doing here?" "I shouldn't be here, but I couldn't call you. I need your help bad MyeZelle! It has to do with my brother Randell. I think he's in a shitload of trouble. How soon can you meet me at the penthouse?" The look in Ron's eyes are both of fear and concern. "Yeah baby, give me an hour, maybe less. Whatever it is, we'll figure it out honey. Just go before the kids get curious and come looking for me." I give Ron a quick hug and disappear back inside.

I locate Natalie in the kitchen. "Hey, that was a client of mine and he needs my services. I'm going to be meeting him downtown and

I have no idea when I'll be back so please see to it that the kids are in bed at a decent hour and I'll be back as soon as I can." "Yes, of course Mrs. M," Natalie responds. After giving the kids quick hugs and kisses, I dash upstairs to retrieve my cell and purse, hop in my car and speed towards downtown.

As I enter the penthouse, I notice Ron first and the guy who escorted me to Ron's private suite who also happens to look a lot like him. "MyeZelle, this is my brother Randell, Randy this is MyeZelle. Uh baby I fixed you a drink. You might need one before we get into why I needed you here now." "Honey, I don't need a drink, I'd really just like to know exactly what is going on." Randell interjects, "I have a friend, I had a friend, Lindsey. She was found dead in her apartment a few weeks ago. The autopsy finally came back and they're trying to say that she overdosed but I don't believe that bullshit!" Randell is full of emotion and Ron has to calm him down. "Look Randy, we can't help if we can't get everything you know out of you. You need to put your emotions to the side and just state the facts so MyeZelle can give us the best advice, alright man?" Randell slowly begins to calm down and picks up where he left off. "Anyway," Randell continues, "Lindsey was in the hospital right before she died! She was pregnant and she swore she wasn't using anymore. She wanted her baby! I was there when she talked to the baby's daddy who ain't shit by the way! She wanted nothing to do with him and he was pissed she was keeping the baby cause he's married with kids. I talked to her after that and she said went to his office and he had a change of heart. He told her he was leaving his wife and kids and him and Lindsey were moving out of state where he got a new job. What man you know gone leave their wife and three or for kids when they got a lot of money they're not trying to part with. I'm telling y'all something ain't right about this shit!"

Ron and I stare at one another other but I'm not sure if they're for the same reason. I pull out my mini recorder and place it on the coffee table. "Okay Randell, I need to record everything to make the proper notes to run by my contacts downtown?" Randell agrees and I start with some very basic questions." "Does she have any family and if so, do you know their names. I will need to contact them to gain access to her apartment if that's still an option and not a crime scene." Randell explains that her family hasn't had anything to do with Lindsey in years. "Her emergency contact was my wife but they had a falling out and when Lindsey went to the emergency room a few weeks ago, she named me as her contact." Now my head is spinning. "Why would she list the two of you? Who were you guys to Lindsey?" Randell goes on to explain his wife and Lindsey were college bff"s and later the three of them engaged in a consensual intimate relationship. Shortly thereafter, Lindsey and Randell had relations without the wife which ended their friendship. "Even though my wife cut Lindsey off, I didn't. My wife was the one who initiated the shit so I would still sneak and see Lindsey. When my wife caught us at our house, she freaked out. She found out Lindsey was seeing this married guy and I think that's who my wife has been hooking up with on some twisted revenge. I think that's what Lindsey was trying to tell me when she was in the hospital. She said the guy was moving to Milwaukee or Memphis. I'm not sure, some city in another state. Anyway, this shit is just not adding up you know. Can't you find out what happened to her?"

I explain to Randell that because Lindsey completed a living Will in the hospital naming him as Executor, we will only need to have it filed in court and can go from there. Randell explains that Lindsey hasn't been buried because her body was only discovered a few days ago after neighbors notice a foul odor coming from her apartment. "She been dead for at least a couple days. I kept trying to call and text her but she would never call or text back. I finally asked my wife had she and Lindsey talked and she lied! Aryah talked to Lindsey last week and they were slowly trying to bet their friendship back. Now, if Lindsey's still her enemy, why in hell has my wife been talking to her! You see why I say there's something going on and its all coming back to my wife and the guy Lindsey was pregnant by. Now you see why I need you help baby, why we need it", Ron pleads.

When Victoria lied to my husband about us having a huge murder case on our hands, I thought I would be able to use that time to spend with Ronald. It now appears as though Victoria has spoken it into existence! "Yes honey, I'm going to do everything I can. I have some contacts in law enforcement as well as the private sector which may be more beneficial to us. They can do things a little differently where ethically, official law enforcement would have to toe the line. The first thing I need to do is get into her place and take a look around. Randell, you and I will head to court first thing in the morning to ensure no one else has tried to claim Executor of her estate. Do you have any idea if her parents are even aware that their daughter and grandchild are dead?" Randell explains that he hasn't spoken with anyone including his wife apart from Ron. The three of us quietly drink and lose ourselves in private thought for more than an hour before I finally break the silence. "Ron, honey, I'm going to bed. Randell, we need to be at court by eight to file the paperwork. I'm hoping to pull enough strings to get everything in order by mid-afternoon and we can gain access to her place." "I'll be right there baby, bro you need to stay with us tonight. Take one of the upstairs rooms or the couch, hell man I don't care but I don't want you going home after you've been drinking with everything that's going on." Randell heeds his brother's advice and stumbles upstairs with Ron following.

"How's Randell doing honey", I ask as Ron enters our bedroom. "He's hurting emotionally for sure. My brother is very hood, very street still and he doesn't show emotions easily or often. I do know that he really cared for this girl and he's suspicious of his wife and this guy I guess they were both seeing. One thing's for sure, if it turns out that she's involved, he's involved or they're both involved, there's going to be bloodshed and I won't be able to do a damn thing about it."

Ron undresses and crawls into bed closely behind me and we fall asleep. Morning came fast and when I opened my eyes, it was already after six. I immediately hop out of bed to take a hot shower. After dressing I find the guys in the kitchen. To my surprise, Ronald is making breakfast. "Good morning," I announce. "Good morning," the guys say in unison. As I sit, Randell turns to me and expresses appreciation for a great job I have yet to work. "No matter how this turns out, I want to thank you now. My brother told me all about you...well almost all about you. I'm know he left out some really good shit," he blurts out with laughter. I can't help but blush as Ron intervenes. "You already know lil bro, if she wasn't A1, I damn sure wouldn't be standing in this kitchen cooking for her fine ass!" We eat breakfast together and Randell I began to leave before Ron stops us. "Listen sweetheart, I don't want you driving your car. My driver is downstairs to take you guys wherever y'all need to go for the day." "If we take him, how are you going to get around honey," I question. Ron looks at me puzzled, "sweetheart, I have three or four cars in the garage, I'll be fine," he laughs. Sensing my nerves are still a bit frayed, Ron whispers in my ear, "don't worry baby. Go take care of the court business and I'll meet you guys wherever else you need to go. Make damn sure you don't go to that apartment without me." With that, he kisses me on the lips and neck and a soft pat on the derriere and Randell and I are out the door.

Court went better than expected. Randell was named Executor of Lindsey's estate, giving him control over Lindsey's medical records, bank accounts, funeral/burial decisions along will all worldly possessions she may have incurred in her short time here. "Well, now that we got that out of the way, we need to contact her parents. As your attorney, I suggest we meet them at their home or my office. Should things go favorably, my suggestion would be to allow the parents access to her apartment to retrieve any items they deem valuable or sentimental to them but only after we have gone through everything thoroughly, got it?!" Randell seemed a bit stunned by my tone and somewhat aggressive demeanor. "Yes ma'am, I got it. My brother right, you don't play," he chuckles.

As Randell makes contact with Lindsey's parents, I make contact with the top detective of Hennepin County's Violent Crime Division, Oscar Vegas. He and I have been friends for over fifteen years, that's not to say that we haven't sparred in that time. He is on one side and I'm on the other, but we have a mutual respect and have worked on other cases together. Right now I need him to help me figure out if this young lady died of an accidental overdose or something more ominous as Randell believes. "Hey Oscar, my client just got off the phone with the young lady's parents and they have agreed to meet with us later this evening at their residence, so are you able to walk through the apartment with us about four?" "Yes, yes, yes MyeZelle, whatever you need, you know that", he replies in the thickest Cuban accent. "Awesome, you're the best," I exclaim!

My focus now shifts back to Randell. In a stern yet motherly voice, I question Randell, "are you sure you're ready for this Randell because you have to understand there's a great probability that we find nothing and this girl had a weak moment that cost her and her child's life." Randell allows my words to soak in before responding. "I get all that, I just want the truth. I know her and she was done with the bullshit I promise you. I wouldn't have dragged you and my brother into this if I thought she slipped. I know somebody behind it, I just don't know who. I could be that nigga. I mean the guy she was pregnant by you know. And this on and off beef with my wife, who knows! We lose ourselves in thought for a few moments before walking in silence to the car.

Randell and I spent the drive over to Lindsey's condo without uttering a word to one another. Thank God radio has evolved into music fitted for individual's personal tastes. I find myself singing and rocking to Raheem DeVaughn's "Just Right". The song ends and I glance over to Randell immersed in his phone on a texting spree. I'm assuming it's his wife as I don't know any man that texts back-to-back! From everything I've learned about Randell, he, his wife, this girl Lindsey have been living a very tangled life!

We finally make it to Lindsey's apartment and as we step in, nothing seems to be out of place. The condo is clean but lived in. "Alright Randell, you know how she moved about her place so think about what her routine was like when you would visit. Before finding out she was pregnant, did Lindsey keep drugs in the house, a specific location, maybe in the bedroom, her closet or a nightstand?" Randell thinks for a few moments, "she didn't really hide her shit, you know what I mean? She really was only into taking an "X" or something like that. She didn't mess with that powder until dude came around. He the one turned Lindsey on to all that other shit. She kept her stuff in this candy dish." The more Randell speaks about the mystery guy, I can feel the rage building inside him. "Okay," I respond with an outstretched hand, "let's just take a few breaths Randell. Oscar will be here in an hour and I would like for us to gather anything you feel may be out of place so let's just focus on that okay?" Randell agrees and we get to work. I have him focus his search on the kitchen and I make my way to the primary bedroom and bath.

Her dresser is filled with cheap perfumes and make-up. All three dresser drawers are filled with bras, panties, socks and tank tops thrown together and unfolded. Finding nothing in the dresser, I hope for better luck with the nightstands on either side of the bed. Bingo, Lindsey kept a journal! I quickly slide that into my briefcase to take a closer look at later and continue my search. After combing through both nightstands with only finding the journal, I check under the bed and find a small caliber handgun along with a recording device. This girl was obviously afraid of someone. A single woman wouldn't keep a handgun under the bed, she would keep it in a gun case for safety. And what woman needs a recording device unless she felt threatened and needed proof. Curiosity is tugging at me to play this recorder now, but I don't give into temptation. I place the gun back where I found it, slip the recording into my briefcase next to the journal and return to the living area.

"You find anything good," Randell questions and I lie. "No, just the normal girly girl stuff. Oh, she does have a handgun under her bed, I'm assuming for protection. Do you know anything about that?" Randell insists Lindsey had the gun to protect herself from the guy she was pregnant by. "Okay, well let's keep looking. Alright, you do a quick run through again of the bedroom in case there's an area I forgot to check out." Randell agrees and I shift my attention to the pillows and cushions on the furniture. Women are almost always losing or stuffing something under a cushion they don't want their husbands or boyfriends to see. I find nothing inside the sofa but underneath, I find a bottle of nasal spray almost completely full. It's the same brand I used for each of my pregnancies for nausea. Lindsey won't be needing this anymore. I was prepared to throw it in the trash but a knock at the door startled me. I toss the spray on the coffee table and gather myself before answering.

"Hey Oscar, thank you so much for coming. Come on in!" "Anything for you cutie pie. So, I guess you've been snooping around before I got here?" Ignoring his cop's intuition, I jump right to it. "So I gave you some insight over the phone." As I'm speaking to Oscar, Randell emerges from the bedroom and quietly sits on the sofa, staring intently at us both. "Oscar, this is Randell, Lindsey's good friend and her Executor I mentioned before. Randell, I was getting Oscar up to speed." Turning my attention back to Oscar, "so what do you think," I question. "Well, let me take a look around. We have a couple hours before meeting the parents so I'll give everything a good once-over." With that, Oscars heads to the bedroom and Randell and I sit in silence. I finally break the silence by turning on the television and ESPN's PTI is blaring through the surround sound. That's when I notice the figurine in the entertainment center has a unique hole in the front of it. I hop out of my seat to grab the "Angel" and as I suspected, there's a hidden camera inside. As Randell stands puzzled at the discovery, I usher him to the kitchen. Whispering, I explain, "there's a hidden camera, find me something to put this in quickly." Randell locates a reusable grocery bag. I place the "Angel" inside and we return to the living area just as Oscar enters.

"Well did you find anything out of the ordinary?" Without responding, Oscar starts a search of the living area. After several minutes of searching, he responds with irritation, "MyeZelle, did you find a video recording device. Before you answer that question, just remember who you're talking to okay?" I'm totally busted but I try to make it sound good. "I was going to turn it over to you after I scanned it. She's a young woman. If it was anything pertinent to her death, you know I would have turned it over to you Oscar," I retort. Oscar doesn't buy my excuse at all! "MyeZelle you know how this works! You asked for my help, let me help. Don't put yourself in a compromising position like this. You will be in the loop of whatever

I find out, both of you. Now, hand over the recorder!" I comply without uttering a word and retake my seat on the sofa next to Randell.

Oscar continued searching the apartment for another hour while Randell returned to a texting spree. I stared blankly at the TV until Oscar finally broke the silence. "So, I found two micro voice recorders. Along with the video recorder, my initial opinion is this girl was in trouble and fearful of someone. I'll have to analyze it when I get in the office tomorrow. Let's lock things up here and head over to her parents' home.

The drive to Edina gave Randell and I an opportunity to discuss the events from the apartment search. "How in hell could he have known there was a camera set up?" Randell turns to me with a puzzled look on his face before responding. "So I guess you don't know nothing about surveillance huh?" Before I have a chance to respond, Randell continues and breaks down exactly how I screwed up. "Well, if you knew that, why didn't you say anything before giving me the bag to take the camera in the first place," I snap back. "I figured you had the drive in your briefcase, it's not like back in the day! You don't need a suitcase to pack the shit up," he shouts back. The boom in his voice frightens me a bit and I remain silent the rest of drive to the Graham's home. I get that he's going through a lot of emotions so I keep my composure and we continue our drive in silence.

Oscar was waiting in the Graham's driveway when we arrived. Undoubtedly, he activated his sirens! Before we're able to exit the car, Oscar walks over to drill us on how to approach Lindsey's family. "We got it Oscar. You're the detective, we're the friends, let them do all the talking, blah, blah, blah!" We reach the front steps as the front door swings open and we're face to face with Lindsey's parents.

We spend the next three hours gaining as much information from the Grahams they were willing to divulge. Oscar was very reserved in sharing information with Lindsey's parents until further information could be obtained. The one thing we all understood, Lindsey's actual life and what her parents knew about were very separate. Because she dated outside of her race, her parents have no interest in attending their daughter's funeral. They have no desire to visit her apartment or retrieve any items from within. They are interested only in knowing if her death was an accidental overdose or murder so the black guy she chose over her family can rot in jail. The Grahams also made it very clear to us they're "absolutely not racist" because they've allowed two blacks and a Hispanic inside their home for repairs. Glad we cleared that shit up!

⌀ Truth to Light-MyeZelle

Randell and I finally make it back to the penthouse to find Ronald waiting for us and he's not happy. "Sweetheart, I asked you to call me so that I could meet y'all over at the apartment, what happened," he questioned. I brush past Ron to drop my purse, keys and pour myself and shot of tequila which I quickly down. After gathering myself, we all sit and I explain to Ronald everything that transpired over the past few hours. "I apologize sweetheart, I was just worried about you and my brother. I mean, yeah I know you two can handle yourselves, I just needed to know that nothing too crazy was going on, that's all baby." "It's alright Ron, we're good and now I'm going to take a bath and head to bed." I give Ron a hug and make my way down the hall to our bedroom. As I walked away, I could hear Ron demanding Randell tells him "everything that happened and don't leave shit out!" I paused for a second but thought the better of it and continued on my way. I'm too mentally exhausted at this point to continue any further conversation.

This bath is everything I need to soothe my body and mind. I'm not sure if there is a such thing as an aching brain, not a headache or migraine but aching, hurting as though there's too much up there at once and my brain needs space to breathe.

I'm not sure how long I was in the bath before Ronald comes in with my cell and a puzzled look. "What's wrong honey," I ask. "Baby, that detective guy you and Ran was with keeps calling your cell. I thought it might be important sweetheart." "Thank you honey, I'll give him a call." With that, my soothing, relaxation time is over! I quickly exit the bath, grab my robe and cell. Once I'm sure Ron and Randell are still in the living area, I close the bedroom door and return Oscar's now seven missed calls.

"Hey Oscar, it's MyeZelle." We weren't supposed to speak until tomorrow so this had better be good as I needed at least another hour in my bath! "MyeZelle, I didn't want to call you tonight but I was interested in what was on those audio and video tapes so I brought them home and played them." Oscar suddenly goes quiet as if he's asked me a question. "Okay Oscar so tell me what's going on?" After another long pause, Oscar continues. "MyeZelle, I brought the tapes home just to get an idea of what this girl was going through. There's a lot on both audio and video. Your husband is on video with this young lady several times. There are things on the tapes that will eventually come to light as I have to turn them in as evidence, I'm really sorry MyeZelle."

I feel my brain seeming to swell at the thought of what may come out of Oscar's mouth next! "Oscar, look, I'm a big girl and I know exactly who my husband is, he's had flings, affairs but we've gotten through those. Please just tell me what exactly if anything I should be worried about!" "MyeZelle, this was more than just a fling with the deceased. According to the audio and videos, she's had at least one abortion at the behest of your husband and became pregnant for a second time. What's more, they're doing drugs, all sorts of drugs, pills, cocaine and that's just the beginning."

Oscar spared me the many details of sexual escapades Keenan and Lindsey engaged in, but he did note that there had been other partners, as in threesomes, foursomes, maybe orgies! The idea that my husband has screwed around yet again doesn't surprise me at all but when you throw in the fact that it's with a dead girl, that's a game changer for sure!

"Oscar, I had no idea he was involved with this woman! Do you think my husband killed her," I ask incredulously! "I'm not sure right now MyeZelle but what I can tell you is, he was at her home the night she died. It's possible she died after he'd already left but that too will have to be investigated. And your friend who was with you tonight was also on a couple of the tapes. You might want to ask what his involvement with Ms. Graham was. Look, I know this is a lot to take in and I'm sorry I had to lay it on you this way but I thought you should know before it gets out." "I need to see those tapes for myself Oscar before you turn them over, please," I beg. "MyeZelle, you know I can't do that! I'm risking my career as it is just by sharing this information with you."

I beg and plead with Oscar for several minutes before he finally relents. After some tears, screaming into a pillow, I get my shit together, throw on a tank and some sweats to confront Randell's ass and lay everything out for Ron before Oscar arrives with the infamous tapes! As I'm leaving the bedroom, I feel this sudden chill all over my body. My legs won't allow me to move and I'm overcome by rage! The emotions racing through my body has my head spinning! Yes, I'm wrong for having an affair! No, I shouldn't look to another man for love and comfort because my husband is no longer interested. I get all of that but this shit right here is beyond me, beyond belief and I want revenge! I actually hope Keenan killed that bitch and he has to spend the rest of his fucking life in prison and he becomes someone's bitch!

I make my way to the living area where Ron and Randell are hanging, watching "Black AF" and having drinks. I ignore them, fix myself a very stiff drink of tequila with a splash of lemon juice. Once I feel the burn in my chest, my shoulders start to relax a bit and I join the guys on the sofa.

Ronald finally breaks the ice. "So, what's up baby, I thought you were going to bed?" "Well, I was going to do just that but decided to return detective Vegas' many missed phone calls and he had some very interesting things to tell me." Ron is confused but my focus is on Randell's ass right now! "Randell, maybe you can enlighten your brother and I on how you know so much about the guy she was seeing?" Randell shrugs his shoulders, "look, I didn't know Lindsey had cameras all over the place. I told you everything already! We have been friends for a while, friends with benefits. She was just in the hospital and was pregnant by some married dude for the second time. He wanted her to get another abortion and she refused. She asked me to help her because he threatened to kill her so I've been going over there to check on her to make sure she was straight. I didn't hurt her. I'm trying to figure out what happened just like your cop friend MyeZelle."

Ron is in complete shock and he's only heard half of this twisted saga. Once Randell has spilled all of his secrets, I'm forced to give them both the "gut punch"! I quickly rush through everything Oscar shared with me, the three of us are all left with blank stares and thoughts. It's too much to take in! "Are y'all serious right now? This is some real life, Will/Jada entanglement type shit to the tenth power man, for real," Ronald exclaims incredulously! I plead with Ron to calm down and he only did so once the concierge rang to ask if it was okay to allow Oscar up.

The three of us take deep breaths along with a quick drink to take some of the ever-increasing edge off. I answer the door for Oscar and invite him in. He immediately recognizes Randell but stopped dead in his tracks after noticing Ron standing off to the side. Oscar whispers, "MyeZelle, I didn't think we would have an audience, you know the situation I'm in!" I persuade Oscar to follow me into the kitchen to have a word. "Oscar, I know the risk you're taking right now and you have to believe and trust me that I would never at any time put your livelihood in jeopardy in any way! I'm safe here and so are you. What happens here tonight between the three of us stays here! What you must do after you leave tonight, I for one don't have any issues with nor do I give a rat's ass anymore. I just need to see the videos for myself, please!" Detective Vegas quickly glances over towards Ron and Randell before turning his attention back to me. "I cannot stress enough the harm that can come to my career and my family MyeZelle, keep your emotions in check and look at this as evidence against a client that a prosecutor would have to turn over to you, this is my fucking life, you know! And another thing, there are too many tapes for you to go over tonight anyway. I brought a couple based on the times recorded, the night the girl died and a couple days before. Trust me, you won't want to see anymore, there's enough on these to make you want to go to take a bath and go to church!"

I take a breath, gather my composure yet again and Oscar and I join the guys in the living area.

Ron got everything set up and returned to his seat next to Randell. Oscar and I sit at the opposite ends of the sofa and we all watch intently. Once the tape ends showing the days leading up to Lindsey's death, everyone remains quiet. Oscar silently hands over the tape depicting the events prior to Ms. Graham's death and as the tape rolls on, my rage increases bit by bit. I know I have to remain calm but seeing the man I once loved with all my being with another woman on film, infuriates me and makes the upcoming decisions I will make all the clearer.

After four plus hours of watching drug fueled sex and the many ménage à trois my soon-to-be ex-husband participated in, I know longer feel hatred, resentment or anger. I feel nothing for him, and I actually feel okay with that! Ron hands over the tapes to Oscar and I walk with him to the elevator to again reassure him that everything we saw tonight and what he did for me is safe with the three of us. Oscar leaves and I return to the penthouse to await Ronald and Randell's reaction.

Unsurprisingly, neither guy utters a word. Ron greets me with a warm, very tight hug and whispers in my ear he will always protect me, and everything is going to work out for me, my children and the both of us, together as a family. As he releases me from his tight grip, I say goodnight to the guys. Tonight, I pray for God to give me peace, strength and resolution to move forward with my children in health, happiness and continued prosperity. It will take a hell of a lot to bring "MyeZelle Lee Macklin" down, and yes, I want my damn maiden name back expeditiously!

✑ Keenan

Man the time has been going by too damn fast! My wife will be here in the next few days so I will have to say goodbye to Aryah, at least until MyeZelle goes back to Minneapolis. She's been a great distraction after sending Lindsey to hell where she belonged! You can't threaten a man's family and expect him to just sit back and give in to your demands. I can't believe the broad ever thought I would actually leave my wife for her! It's more satisfying to know that no one is going to miss that bitch! I was the last one on her team and now that she's gone, I won't ever have to worry about a love child!

Justin decided to lease the property next door which works out even better than him living with me and the kids over the summer. Aryah can now stay with J whenever she comes to town. I've asked her to move to Memphis permanently with me with but she hasn't budged to this point. Her husband still has a grip on her but I can tell I'm wearing her down. I need her at my disposal ready to take care of any needs I may have or come up with. I'm sure in the back of her mind could be the treatment I doled out to her former friend! Aryah is different though, she has class and more mature than Lindsey. I'll be able to show her off here in the Bluff City without getting caught up and when wifey comes to town, she'll know to stay in her lane. If I can get her down with what I got going on, she won't find herself in that position! But, I will make that bitch disappear the moment she acts up just like Lindsey if I need to! She has to know that I'm that "Man", I run shit and when Zelle gets here, her ass is gonna know it too! "All these women better recognize who I really am, "I'm that man, I'm the king of all my castles," I mutter to myself!

After downing five shots of Hennessey, I start dialing numbers but no one is answering. "Hey J, what's up man?" Finally, I get a voice on the phone! "What up Kee," Justin responds dryly. Maybe it's the Henney got me thinking my boy sounding shady so I dismiss the thought. "What's up man, I was thinking we should hit Beale Street tonight, see what's up. I wanna see what these southern thick girls like before MyeZelle gets here." After a brief pause, Justin blows me off. "Man Kee, I don't know where you get the energy or the balls to keep doing the bullshit you do but I really don't want no more parts of what you got going on! Do you not realize you killed a bitch over some jealousy type shit and you're married! You really killed that girl and so far you're hands are clean but I wouldn't keep pushing my luck! I mean do you not fucking get that shit!" Before I can interject, Justin continues, "It's bad enough you did what you did. Now you're talking about bringing another broad down here that also happens to be married by the way. Your kids will be here for the summer and you still want to go out and chase more pussy?!" Justin continues to berate me. "I don't know if it's your natural ego, the money we making now, the fucking drugs you do with these skank hoes or the fact that you're an undercover "MAGA" loving nigga but I'm not co-signing no more of your bullshit! You're still a black man that killed a white woman! Dude, you can wake up now before it's too late or hit up one of them Shapiro dudes to be your flunky cause I'm not about to let you take me down with your dumb shit! If it ain't about work Kee or about you seeing the light and coming to your fucking senses, don't call me!"

I can't believe my best friend, my business partner, my brother just tried to chastise me! Who the fuck does he think he is? How dare that dude speak to me that way! "J, you know what man, all this sensitive shit you going through right now, I mean, why? Cause your wife turned out to be a greedy, socialite wannabe bitch, who played you, huh J?! You know what man, I've been drinking so I'm gonna stop talking, I'll holla at you in the morning man when we both feel better, love!" I hang up before giving Justin a chance to respond. Maybe I did take the shit the wrong way. Maybe I did drink too much but a grown man who provides for his family should be able to do whatever the hell he wants!

I fall asleep completely clothed to the sound of my cell ringing off the hook! Damn, I have a headache. I was so frustrated with Justin last night; I didn't bother to order takeout or delivery and now I'm paying the price for it. My cell continues to blow up so I finally grab it to see my wife has called me five times!

After taking a cold shower to get my head right, I finally call my number one Queen. "Hey sweetheart, I'm sorry I missed your calls last night, what's up baby?" MyeZelle takes a long sigh before responding, "well Keenan, there are a lot of things up right now. We won't be coming to Memphis due to all the quarantine restrictions happening right now so I think it would be safer if you would come home when your schedule allows." Damn, my baby sounds too calm and a little cold to me but maybe it's just this hangover I'm dealing with. "Okay baby, well let me try to get things in order here and I'll give you a call back later today so I can let you know what's up and talk to the kids." Before I can say I love you, talk to you later, MyeZelle clicked on me! It has to be the Henney from last night cause shit not feeling right at all! It was enough that my brother, Justin has turned on me, now my wife is ghosting!

After a long, hot shower to get my mind right, I reach out to Justin, hoping for a better outcome from our last conversation. "J, what's up man?" I receive a very dry response but not deterred. "Listen J, I need to catch a flight home tonight, there's something going on with Mye and the kids. She's not allowing the kids to come anymore and didn't give me an explanation." "Kee, man, you know

163

it's lockdowns all over the country. Maybe she feels like it's better for you to travel versus her and the kids traveling back and forth, you know what I mean?"

Justin tries to reassure me that everything is fine with MyeZelle and she's just protecting our children's health with everything that's going on with this pandemic. I'm not buying what he neither MyeZelle is selling. I assure J I will be back in a couple days and end the call. My world is getting out of control and I have to get back on my square! I know I've put myself in this situation but I'm more than capable of fixing it, cause that's what I've always done!

I give Shapiro a call to let him know Justin will be in charge for the next few days so I can check on things back home. He's very understanding and offers his private plane to get me into Minneapolis tonight, I quickly and graciously accept.

I don't bother to pack any clothing, only a carry-on to hold a shaving kit with my briefcase. While waiting on the driver for pick-up, I stare down at the few people walking along Beale Street. I was told Beale is normally bustling with tourists along with locals no matter the day or time. But tonight, it's mostly quiet. Some couples holding hands, ladies appearing to have a girls' night out and single guys looking to get lucky. My thoughts are interrupted by hotel phone ringing, and I don't bother to answer. It's the concierge notifying me the driver is here. I quickly gather my things and head for the elevator.

The ride to Memphis International was short and uneventful. I'm on Shapiro's private plane and in the air within an hour. As per usual, Shapiro has a hot stewardess waiting on my beck and call but I'm completely lost in my thoughts and wave her off. With less than two hours in the air, I don't have a need for food or drink. My stomach is turning so food or drink would only fuck it up more! Outside of having a car waiting to get me to my destination, I don't need anything else.

The plane ride was smooth and the drive home was just as smooth so why am I so uneasy and nervous! All of the lights are out as expected, it's after one in the morning. As I make my way to the master suite, I can hear the tv clearly airing a Real Housewives show, my wife's up this late? "Hey sweetheart," I say softly. MyeZelle glares at me, without uttering a word, she brushes past me and closes the bedroom door.

"Well, Mr. Washington, it's good that you made it home, this way I can tell you in person." I'm hella confused, I have no idea what my wife is about tell me but my legs are starting to quiver. "What's going on baby," I question. "GOD please," I beg and pray to myself, "please do not let one of these side hoes be the reason for this late night pow-wow!" MyeZelle walks over to her nightstand and lights up a Newport! A Newport cigarette, this woman hasn't smoked in well over ten years! As she smokes her cigarette, I remain silent. The entire time, she's staring me up and down. I suddenly have an urge to excuse myself to the bathroom. I'm in there for at least twenty minutes to get myself together. Whatever my wife has to tell me, it's not good and I'm terrified of just how bad it's going to be. Once I exit the bathroom, she's waiting in full on bitch mode!

"So, Mr. Washington, I'm going to make this as short and to the point as possible because my children are sleeping and I don't want any bullshit." Did Mye just say "my children", as in "her children" and not "our children", thinking to myself. MyeZelle continues, "our marriage is over Keenan. I want a divorce and I would expect you to cooperate fully without any push-back." "MyeZelle, have you lost your fucking mind, what do you mean?" She lays it all out for me and I feel like I've just been on episode of "Cheaters"!

As I deny and be and plead, my wife isn't interested in anything I'm throwing her way. "Keenan, you don't understand. There are video tapes of you and your bitch, excuse me your bitches but more importantly, I have copies of said tapes in a very safe location. On one of those tapes, you're in that hooker's apartment the night she overdosed, committed suicide or murdered! Interestingly enough, you left an item behind that I'm sure Minneapolis PD will be very interested in testing. For your sake, you best hope that girl's autopsy doesn't contain more drugs than a human body can consume before dying. You see, I have your black ass by the balls. Now, do you see how this is going and will go!"

I have no idea how much time went by before I was able to speak again. "MyeZelle, baby, I'm so sorry! I swear to you Mye, I will do anything, whatever it takes baby, I promise. I'll go to marriage counseling, church, whatever you want. We can renew our vows, you know, start fresh. Please baby, I'll do anything to save our marriage. I'm so sorry." I get down on my knees at my wife's feet but she's undeterred. "The only thing you can do Keenan right now is get the fuck out of my house! As I said, when you come to visit our children, you are to give me a twenty-four-hour notice so I can prepare not to be here. We have nothing more to discuss outside of finances for a divorce. Now, as quietly as you crept your disgusting ass in this house, leave the same way! We're done!"

MyeZelle walks back to her nightstand, and I finally get off my knees. I stare nowhere for a while trying to come to grips with what just happened. Hours ago, I was in Memphis thinking about the next side piece I could get. Now I'm standing in my bedroom having just lost the best thing that's ever happened to me. Tears begin to roll down my face, but my despair is rudely jerked backed to reality! "Did you not hear me the first or second time Keenan fucking Washington? Get the fuck out of my home or I will be forced to open this drawer and use this "Nine" to permanently remove you from our lives. Hell at this point, it would be my pleasure, get out now!" My wife is deadly serious and I turn without saying a word to leave. I've pressed my luck too many times and now it has finally run out!

꒰ MyeZelle

Keenan is back in Memphis and the children and I are enjoying our new normal. They talk with their father each night with the understanding that their dad is working out-of-state. We have agreed to allow some time to pass before sitting our children down and explaining the new dynamic of family life, life that will no longer include their father and I together. Separating a family can have devastating affects on children and I want to ease the pain and anxiety almost sure to come along with that as much as possible.

With Keenan now coming in every other weekend, it has been a bit trying. I've had to make up reasons as to why I'm working out of town each weekend he's home and the twins are starting to question each of us as time passes. The truth is, I'm not out of town at all, I'm with Ronald. Each visit Kee has made since our "come to Jesus" moment, as he walks in the door, I walk out. No exchange of pleasantries, just strangers passing by one another.

We have scheduled a vacation to Myrtle Beach, booking a comfortable AirBnB for an end-of-the summer getaway for the children. I packed the week with as many activities I could find due to the restraints the pandemic is having on the country. If nothing else, I'm committed to lying on the beach from sunup to sundown to be away from Kee. The thought of having him in my presence for a week is utterly making me sick to my stomach. I don't have hate any longer for him, it's that I have absolutely nothing left for him. Once you have given your all to someone who doesn't reciprocate, it doesn't take long for your emotional connection to dissipate entirely and that's where I am!

I'm packing my overnight bag as Keenan will be here any moment. We are scheduled to leave for Myrtle Beach Sunday night so tonight and tomorrow will be the only time I have to spend with Ron for a week. I'm lost in thought when I feel a hand on my shoulder that causes my entire body to stiffen. I instantly turn, and it's Keenan. "What is it Keenan", I demand! His eyes are dark underneath and he's lost a considerable amount of weight upon quick inspection. "I'm sorry MyeZelle, I didn't mean to startle you. I was just hoping we could talk before you rush out the door." "We have nothing to talk about Keenan, unless you've signed the divorce papers that's been sitting collecting dust for weeks! Have you signed the papers Keenan?" He remains calm, "no I haven't signed the papers, I don't want to sign the damn papers Mye, I want to work this out, I want us to work out. Baby please, all I'm asking is for one last chance Mye," he begs. "You've had more chances than ten cats with nine lives, I have to go." I grab my things and make my way to the garage quietly without waking my children. As I back my way out of the driveway, Keenan comes out and glares with a look of hatred I've never seen before!

I finally make it to the penthouse and Ron is of course waiting. He's gotten the mood right with fresh pink, red and white roses in two feet vases everywhere! And he's playing my favorite singer of all time, "Johnnie Taylor"! We had a prior conversation about our favorite musical artists while getting to know one another but this man knows absolutely nothing about the legendary blues singer that was "Johnnie Taylor"! He's literally pulling out all the stops for this weekend!

"Hey sweetheart," Ron says with a warm hug and kiss on the forehead. "Hey yourself my honey love," I respond. "So, I was going to fix our favorite meal but the only thing I'm hungry for is you. I fixed you a drink baby." "Sounds good honey, let me just get out of these clothes and slip into something a little more comfortable." While I briskly walk towards the bedroom, I can faintly hear Ron trying to sing along to "Sending You A Kiss". I bet he's been practicing on that shit all day, smiling to myself.

I'm back in a flash and this chocolate, cocoa brown, tall, built fine ass man is lounging on the sofa completely nude now listening to the "O"Jays"! "I wasn't expecting this when I returned!" As I walk over to Ron, my pelvis starts to ache, sharp, sensual pains shooting through my throbbing pussy. "Take everything off baby and come to me," he demands. I oblige and snuggle next to my man.

While music plays in the background, Ron spends several minutes massaging my feet as I sip on a margarita. He slowly rises and places my right leg over the sofa. He kneels and spreads my lips. The second his tongue kisses my clit; I begin to quiver. Ron ignores my pleas begging him to stop, grabbing my hips and sucking my pussy until I'm out of juices and breath! He wastes no time in placing his strong, thick rock-hard dick into me and my mind and body both are completely and utterly drained by the time he cums!

⟨ᖰ **Keenan**

Yeah, I followed my wife tonight! She was so busy trying to get away from me, she didn't notice I was right behind her ass! She can't lie any longer and tell me she's staying with Vic while I'm home with our kids! I walk in the door, there's some punk standing behind a desk smiling as though he knows me, so I play along. "Hey, how you doing," I muster. "I'm trying to surprise my sister and her new husband. I just made it back from another tour oversees and I want to meet my new brother-in-law," I lie! "Well sir, what is your sister's name, and I can ring her or the new husband if they're in?" Did this punk not just hear what I said, I want to surprise them! "Her name is MyeZelle Washington, and her husband's name is."

Before I could finish my sentence, he replies, "oh yes Mrs. Washington, she's so amazing, always smiling and so happy! Her new husband clearly has her glowing! I'm so excited you're here to share that with her," he exclaims! "Yeah, yeah but I don't want you to ring her, I want to surprise her, you know what I mean?" "Unfortunately sir, I'm unable to do that. I could lose my job. It's a confidentiality thing. That's why our tenants pay the big bucks for this place. I could never live here. just work here." I cut him off. "Okay, I understand and it's getting late anyway, and I have to unpack, it was a long flight you know what I mean. So tell you what, don't let her know I was here and tomorrow I'll come back and bring my baby sis a special gift okay?" the concierge agreed and with that I leave.

So my wife has a side nigga? Did MyeZelle really think I wasn't going to find out? I have a rude awakening for her and dude she's been sleeping with. I got something for that bitch and him!

After returning home and checking on my babies I retreat to the family room. I won't ever sleep in the master bedroom again. It wouldn't surprise me if the bitch had her side dick in our home, in our bed while our children were asleep down the hall! I waste no time putting my plan in motion.

"So yeah J, like I was saying man, I'm sending a package to you in the morning cause it looks like I might be here for a while." After a long pause, Justin finally responds, "Kee, I know things seem messed up right now, you just gotta take a breath. You've done a bunch of shit to your wife, the whole time y'all been married. You're worried about the wrong thing brother. What you need to do is beg and plead for your wife's forgiveness and pray she takes your raggedy ass back, eventually! You killed a woman you were screwing and MyeZelle knows everything now, yet you're focused on her getting a piece of dick after all that? Grow up Kee!" I don't understand how my brother, my best friend is siding with my wife. What the hell happened to "bros before hoes"?! Justin continues his rant. "The best thing you can do brother is repair the damage you created to bring this situation to where it is today. Do whatever you have to do to save your marriage and your family. You have to give MyeZelle the times she needs. She'll realize that keeping the family together is what's best. That's the best advice I can give you brother!" We converse a while longer and before ending the call, I remind J to look for my package.

☙ Hell Has No Fury

It's after 2AM before I finalize my plans and drift off to sleep. Tomorrow is going to be a big day in all our lives. I don't sleep for long, I wake before five but I'm energized and ready to go!

Though I had no intentions of ever entering our marital bedroom again, I have to get the supplies I need to handle business today. The kids are still sleeping and I make my way downstairs to give Rosie instructions for the day. "So Mr. Washington, what should I prepare for dinner tonight?" "Well Rosie, I think you should make something special for the kids, get their favorite meals together. You know, since we're going to be away for a week, I want them to enjoy that great cooking you put together for us every day." "Okay, I will do that, is there anything I can prepare for you?" I decline and proceed to the garage.

As I stand in the middle of my garage, I contemplate my next steps and ponder if I'm really ready for this. Once I leave, there is no turning back. The drive seems longer today but it gave me time to think about my life, my children, Justin, my wife, my life! On the way over, I stopped to pick up three dozen roses, all white. White is angelic right? After arriving downtown, I park a block away and suit up. Upon entering the building, I see the same guy from last night. He's smiling and before he speaks, a couple gunshots rang out and he's down, two to the head! I quickly round the desk and check the tenant registry. Got it!

As I make my way to the elevator, my heart is racing, and my adrenaline is through the roof but there's no turning back now! The roses have a little bit of blow-back blood so I try as best as I can to mask the drippings. The elevator opens and once I step out,

I take a moment to inhale/exhale a couple deep breaths. I ring the doorbell and a very deep voice responds. "I have flowers for a Mrs. Washington sir," I respond. Upon opening the door, I immediately fire three shots in quick succession!

I hear noise coming from the back of the condo and make my way down the hall. As I round the corner to the master bedroom, I'm struck on the head with something and immediately hear voices!

"Baby use that gun, shoot him," the guy screams! Out of the corner of my eye, I can see my wife holding a handgun. I struggle to get up and the guy I'm wrestling around with looks like the same guy I took out seconds ago. We're wrestling and I'm doing my best to take him, but this nigga is strong and I fall in and out of consciousness from the blow to the head!

I faintly hear my wife arguing with the someone as I regain consciousness. I'm assuming the guy who just whipped my ass! "Why would I want to kill him Ron? Enough has been done, the police are on the way, and I would much rather his ass go prison for life and suffer than make it easy for him by putting a bullet in his brain. Think this through baby," she pleads! My wife is begging a man to spare my life?!

Minutes before the cops arrive, I'm able to sit halfway up and standing over me is my wife and this big nigga that was trying to kill me! "MyeZelle," I beg, "you're my wife, you have to help me!" As she glares at me with ice-cold eyes, she responds, "I helped you by sparing your life so our children will know exactly what has taken place! I could have blown you away and didn't. I have something better for you, you're going to prison for life, Keenan and my children and I are moving on without you!" Before I can respond, radios, detectives and cops are surrounding us!

"Put the gun down ma'am," a detective is demanding while holding his gun. MyeZelle complies and the three of us are handcuffed and moved into the living area where the other guy lays dead! The detectives order cops to transport the three of us downtown while they sort out the carnage I left behind. I demand medical attention but to no avail. I'm placed in an interrogation room after being stripped of clothing, shoes, and given a plastic suit to put on, along with a towel to nurse my bleeding lip and nose. Two detectives enter the room and I immediately lawyer up, nothing to say!

✎ Hell Has No Fury

This isn't happening! Keenan has lost his freaking mind! How and why are the only things going through my mind at this point! I request detective Vegas and after several hours of waiting, he finally enters. "Oh, thank GOD Oscar. I've been sitting here for hours," I exclaim! "I apologize MyeZelle, I had to cover the crime scene. I know this is a lot. Just take your time and tell me everything you can remember, okay?"

I explain to Detective Vegas, "Ron and I we're in our bedroom asleep. Randell must have come in after we had gone to bed. The next thing I remember is hearing gunshots. I wasn't sure but Ron knew immediately and jumped out of bed. He grabbed a gun, passed it to me and retrieved a bat from his closet. Ron was waiting for whoever it was and as he attempted to enter our room, Ron hit him in the head with the bat and they began to fight. That's when I realized it was Keenan! I had no idea he knew about my place Oscar, I promise! I can't believe this is real right now!"

Detective Vegas calms me as much as I can be calmed at this point and I continue. "I grabbed the gun Keenan had, threw it across the room from both guys and once Keenan was down, I called 911 while holding Ron's gun on my husband." Oscar explains that Randell isn't dead but in grave condition and may not make it. Keenan killed our concierge to gain access to his computer, thus finding the floor of my residence. "Listen MyeZelle, your friend, boyfriend whatever he may be is in some trouble at this point. He's not allowed to own a firearm. So, I need to ask you, who's the owner of the gun Mr. Henderson had handy when all this occurred?" Without blinking, I claimed the gun, I took ownership of the gun. Though Detective Vegas knew I had lied, the gun never became a factor.

Keenan was charged with first degree murder, first degree attempted murder along with two counts of wanton assault with intent to create bodily harm.

After months of preliminary hearings, continuances, Keenan finally pled guilty to avoid a trial. He was sentenced to thirty-five years to life. In that time, our divorce became final.

Randell was hospitalized for three months and is now in rehab. He must learn to talk, walk and eat again but he's a fighter and making great progress.

After many therapy sessions with my children to get through this entire ordeal, they are also healing from the trauma of what their father did and where he will be for potentially the remainder of his life.

The package Keenan sent to Justin in Memphis the night before he went on a rampage was turned over to me. Keenan sold his share of his and Justin's company for one dollar to Justin. Knowing what he was going to do the next day, he still had the wherewithal to try and screw not just me but our children! Thank God Justin has a conscientious! J sold the company back to me for $2! Once the red tape was all clear, I sold Keenan's half to Justin for a fair and reasonable price which we were both happy with.

Justin divorced his once Amish turned socialite of a wife and I graciously represented him! She moved out of state and landed in LA, go figure!

Victoria and Gary are actually making a go of their relationship, it's awesome! The four of us are basically inseparable now. We spend a lot of time at my penthouse and my kids love it! Yes, Bonnie and Clyde are right here with us as I sold my once marital home to Rosie and her sister, for you guessed it one dollar! Rosie still takes care of us three nights out the week, but I've cut my schedule drastically from the office. Vic and I made a decision to hire another attorney part-time to feel in the gaps. I'm here with my four babies as we navigate the next phase of our lives.

The year 2020 was hell to say the least! Now that 2021 has come, we have all settled into our new normal.

Life is what you make it! The moral of my story is this: no matter how hard life gets with the one you love, fight for it or let it go! Never get so wrapped up in yourself that you only think about yourself! Otherwise, you may just find yourself wrapped in a deadly entanglement!!!

CPSIA information can be obtained
at www.ICGtesting.com
Printed in the USA
BVHW071627120122
625993BV00005B/668